WHAT IF...

You were a wild sea otter.
and something bad
happened to you, but
you ended up in a cozy sea park.

You made some great friends
that you loved with all your heart.

THEN YOU REALIZED...

IT'S TIME
TO GO HOME.

But your friends
couldn't join you.

WHAT WOULD YOU DO?

COULD YOU HAVE YOUR SQUID AND EAT IT, TOO?

Ollie the Otter

Kelly Alan Williamson

Talking Critters™ series

Published by Cherubs Play ™
Talking Critters ™ series
PO BOX 2817, Yountville, CA 94599, USA
www.cherubsplay.com

Book Design: Peri Poloni, Knockout Design,www.knockoutbooks.com

Publisher's Cataloging-in-Publication
(Provided by Quality Books, Inc.)

Williamson, Kelly, Alan.
Ollie the Otter / Kelly Alan Williamson. - 1st ed.
p. cm. - (Talking critters series)

SUMMARY: A sea otter gets caught by a fisherman and is brought to a nearby sea park where he befriends the other animals there. Before his planned release he convinces the domestic "lifers" to escape with him to his home and experience life on the wild side.

Audience: Ages 8-up.
LCCN 00-110620
ISBN 0-9706467-0-4

1. Sea otter-Juvenile fiction. 2. Escapes-Juvenile fiction. I. Title.

PZ7.W6723O11 2001 [Fic]
QBI00-902096

Printed in the United States of America

10 9 8 7 6 5 4 3 2 1

For Christina, Jessie, and Sean, who heard this story first.

To my spiritual preceptor by whose grace everything is possible.

DISCLAIMER

While the author took great pains to research and portray otters and their natural habitat, this book is pure-fun fiction and its purpose is to entertain. The names of these make-believe characters do not represent any specific, known, or otherwise living animals. The names and descriptions of the fictitious places in this book do not represent any actual public aquarium, museum, zoo, or wildlife park. The author and publisher shall have neither liability nor responsibility to any person or entity with respect to any loss or damage caused, or alleged to have been caused, directly or indirectly, by the information contained in this book.

Contents

CHAPTER 1

Otter Rock

Not long ago there was a wonderful place for marine animals to live called Otter Rock. Sea otters frolicked there in peace for years, feasting on abalone and other tasty seafood.

The leader of the local teenage otters was a rough and tumble guy named Ollie.

One day Ollie and some of his friends ventured to an area they were not supposed to be — the far side of Otter Rock. They'd heard startling news from a pelican which prompted them to make the journey.

"A great white shark, deader than dead can get," gossiped the gawky brown bird. "A big one, belly-up on the bottom."

The rumor grew until the tale was told that Tooth the great white shark was dead, brought to his death by a horde of vigilante otters.

On Otter Rock, Tooth was known as the meanest and ugliest predator in the Pacific.

The giant shark would cruise the outer kelp beds and taunt with a wicked laugh, "An otter a day keeps my tapeworm at bay! Ha, ha-ha-ha, haaaaaa!"

Tooth would then disappear into the dark emptiness of deep water and wait for the otters to forget. And forget they would, since they were happy and had much good food to eat. The most delicious of which was the red abalone, found in the depths of Tooth's domain.

Sooner or later an otter would swim past the safety of the kelp and Tooth would strike suddenly and viciously. But now, Tooth was dead. It would be fun and safe for the otters to ditch their parents and make their secret journey.

The otters arrived at the backside of Otter Rock and flirted at the edge of the outer kelp, near the dangerous open water.

"Who wants to look for the dead shark with me?" asked Ollie.

None of the otters volunteered.

"Okay," pressed Ollie. "Who thinks they can dive as deep as

I can?"

None accepted the challenge.

"Well, then I'll tell you never-knowers how it looks when I get back. Humphhh."

Ollie swam past the last kelp ribbons and dove into the dark water. He kicked his way to the bottom and looked all around. There was no dead anything, let alone Tooth the great white shark. *What a terrible rumor,* thought Ollie. *And what a bunch of bottom feeders we were to believe it.*

Ollie shot to the top quickly. All of his pals were lounging in the kelp leaves, rolled up like surf rats in blankets, snacking on brown turban snails.

"There's no dead Tooth!" shouted Ollie. "Not even a little blue shark. What a bunch of calamari!"

"Ahh, don't get your fur all matted up or you'll sink," said one of Ollie's friends.

"I otter flap that pelican's baggy throat for leading us on like that," responded Ollie.

But he soon got caught up in otter games and forgot about the pelican and the dead shark that was supposed to be.

The otters were too busy being otters and didn't realize how close a harvesting boat had come to Otter Rock. When they finally paid attention they saw a huge black eel, with a mouth as big as a shark's, being lifted over the side of the boat and into the water. Some men in yellow slickers held onto the giant eel.

"Whoa!" shouted Ollie. "I've never seen an eel that big!"

"Let's get a closer look!" urged one of his pals.

"I don't know," cautioned a third otter. "That thing looks dangerous."

"Last one to the bottom is a mud sucker!" exclaimed Ollie.

The otters dove under the water. They watched as the slithering monster sucked everything off the ocean bottom. Urchins, abalone, rocks, starfish, everything. Two big shiny blades, that were somehow connected to the eel and looked like monster crab claws, sliced the kelp stalks at their roots. The big black eel inhaled the underwater forest as if the heavy kelp plants were weightless. Wherever the big eel moved, nothing was left, except for barren ocean bottom.

"Hey, you're taking away all our food," said Ollie.

Ollie swam up to the eel and punched it, then darted back, looking to see if it would come after him.

But the eel didn't seem to notice Ollie. It kept devouring everything in sight and was about to inhale a prized bed of urchins.

"Oh no you don't," yelled Ollie, as he dove for the tasty morsels, gathering as many as he could before the eel could get them.

Ollie was suddenly swept off his hindflippers and sucked into the mouth of the eel. The other otters watched in horror as the big black eel swallowed Ollie and the urchins in one gulp.

CHAPTER 2

Belly of the Black Eel

Ollie heard a loud vibrating noise as he was pulled deeper into the eel's mouth. He raked his claws at the sides of the giant snake-monster's throat, but couldn't hold on. He was being sucked down faster and faster and couldn't see where he was going. Finally the eel's throat exploded with a loud pop sound, like a stubborn abalone broken free from its shell.

Ollie slammed, back-side first, into a bunch of sharp needles and was blinded for an instant by a bright light.

Ollie's vision adjusted quickly to the twelve o'clock sun directly over his head. He saw that he was in a huge tub with thousands of urchins, hundreds of abalone, and starfish and kelp everywhere. *This isn't the eel's belly after all,* thought Ollie.

Suddenly, something grabbed the nape of his neck from behind and lifted him out of the tub.

"Well, well, well. Whadda we got here?" said a big man with a red face.

"Throw the scraggly mutt overboard!" shouted another man with a thick, black beard, and black cap. "Help me move the suction hose."

"In a minute," said Red Face. "I'm gonna get a lot of money for this little guy. Lotta money."

"No market for otters. We got real work to do. Understand?"

"Yeah, right," groaned Red Face.

Red Face wiped some blood that trickled from one of Ollie's forepaws. He looked closely at Ollie's wound.

"Hope you're not damaged goods."

He inspected Ollie's other paw and both hindflippers.

"At least these are okay. Worse comes to worse, I can cut that one toe off."

Ollie bit the man's hand as hard as he could.

"Ouch!" yelled Red Face, grabbing Ollie's jaw. "You do that again and you'll wish cutting a toe off is all I do!"

Ollie tried to bite Red Face again, but was restrained by the mean man. Red Face opened a storage container that held some fish and crabs and threw Ollie inside. Ollie looked up with pleading eyes as the man was about to shut the lid.

"Don't give me that puppy look," said Red Face, as he closed the container.

Inside, it was mostly dark, except for strips of light piercing in through air holes. The container was only slightly higher than Ollie was tall but it was long and wide.

Ollie crawled, favoring his hurt paw, over to a corner and curled up next to a big halibut. The flatfish's eyes didn't move. Ollie touched it with the tip of his left hindflipper. The halibut remained stiff. From another corner a rock crab broke free from a tangle of look-alikes and scuttled towards Ollie.

With big eyes poking out from its shell, the rock crab piped up, "It's dead. They're all dead. And you'll get boiled too if you don't get out of here!"

"Boiled?"

"You don't want to know, man," said the crab.

"Survivors get blisters just talking about it," spoke another crab. "If you promise not to eat us, we'll help you get out of here."

Ollie looked around the container. He gulped nervously, seeing hundreds of crab peepers and the many lifeless fish eyes, staring at him.

"Weasel face ain't giving you an answer!" blurted a crab from the family heap.

"Yeah," yelled another, closing his claws into horny fists.

"Get ready to rumble!" shouted yet another crustacean.

"Relax crabs," said Ollie. "I'm scared just like you. I won't eat you."

"I don't know," said a crab from the cluster. "The otter could pick us off one at a time."

"We've got no choice," said the lead crab. "Let's hope he's a mammal of his word."

"I don't even like crabs," explained Ollie. "I mean to eat."

"Oh yeah," said a crab from the pile. "Then what do ya eat?"

"Purple and red sea urchins, brown turban snails, squid — when my mom gets them for me, and red abalone is my favorite."

"Okay," said the lead crab, turning to his clan. "I say this otter's clean."

The lead crab then motioned with his claw for Ollie to come closer. Ollie leaned his head forward.

"Me and my pals have got a plan," said the crab. "We're gonna do a standard stack-up and flip-out."

"Maybe you can help with the getaway," offered another crab.

"Let's make the otter feel like he's part of the team," said the lead crab.

The multitude of other crabs all waved a claw.

"Hi," said one of them, then another, and yet another, until all the crabs had welcomed Ollie.

Ollie tried to smile but couldn't. The crabs and their escape plan didn't concern him. Right now he had no idea where he was and all he'd ever heard about humans was that they weren't any good. The many dead fish and nervous, day-dreaming rock crabs, only reaffirmed his fears.

"Like I was saying," said the lead crab. "We're gonna bust out of this joint. No problem. Let me give ya the details."

Just then the latch to the lid clanked against its steel hasp.

"Now!" yelled the crab, as he raced back to the heap and scuttled to the top.

"Hey, you jabbed my eyeball!" groaned a crab at the bottom of the pile.

"You stepped on my feeler!" cried another crab.

"Why do you get to be on top?" demanded a third crab, as the lid slid back and daylight cascaded into the container.

Ollie huddled in the corner watching. *Would this crazy plan work?* he wondered.

The crab on top of the crustacean heap reached for the lip of the container and grabbed hold firmly.

He's going to make it, thought Ollie.

But the crab in second position jealously yanked on the leader's hind leg. The lead crab lost his precarious balance and fell end over end to the bottom, breaking a feeler in the process. All the crabs began greedily pulling on each other and clawing to get to the top.

Ollie shook his head. *This entire pile of arguing crabs is doomed to stay in the container*, he thought.

Sure enough, the tower of crabs collapsed leaving the crazy crustaceans scurrying for cover under dead fish.

Red Face suddenly appeared and looked into the container. His hand was bandaged. He stared at Ollie who was curled up in the corner.

"Here's an abalone. Let's see a happy face, will ya. Nobody's gonna buy an otter with a scowl."

The man jammed a wedge under the big abalone, freeing the sweet meat from the shell. He threw the food into the container, yet Ollie stayed in the corner.

"Well," asked the man. "Aren't ya gonna dig in?"

Ollie remained cautious, keeping a sharp eye on Red Face. Ollie wasn't going to eat with him watching.

"You'll chow down when ya get hungry enough," grunted Red Face, as he closed the lid.

Ollie felt scared and all alone.

CHAPTER 3

The Deep Blue Sea

The container was darker now so Ollie figured it must be night. He missed his mom and dad and knew they would be worried. Ollie was more concerned about how upset they would be than he was afraid for himself. He loved his parents. No matter what, Ollie vowed he would do everything possible to make it back to Otter Rock.

Ollie licked the dried blood off his hurt paw. *What was going to happen next,* he wondered? He realized he could at least do something positive by saying a prayer. He prayed to the Deep Blue Sea, asking that somehow, some way, he would make it back home.

All otters knew there was an essence that permeated the ocean. They called this essence 'the Deep Blue Sea' and understood that it operated without apparent reason and could be invoked for luck and genuine wishes. The Deep Blue Sea had saved many an otter from sharks. Its warning came like a divine hint in a warm current, making an otter move just in time to avoid the sharp teeth of a shark.

The otters always said a prayer before swimming out into the channel to eat squid. Not all otters returned from such food trips, but that was also part of the Deep Blue Sea's divine plan. Just as the otters gorged themselves on hundreds of spawning squid, sometimes otters got eaten so other creatures could live, even if the other creatures were sharks.

Great white sharks and humans were the otters' primary enemies. Otters didn't know much about humans, and therefore, didn't understand them. But they knew all about great whites. Although the otter's loved ones were sometimes eaten, they didn't hate sharks. Otters understood that sharks had their place in the Deep Blue Sea's scheme. But that didn't stop the otters from rafting in the kelp and telling shark jokes.

Ollie had been taught by his mom and dad to thank the Deep Blue Sea for all his good fortune, before going to sleep. Tonight, he finished his prayer by thanking the mysterious force that he wasn't in the belly of a giant eel. Ollie closed his tired eyes and fell asleep licking his sore paw.

CHAPTER 4

Kris

The pounding of the boat against the dock woke Ollie. Through the darkness, Ollie could see the many dead fish in the container had lost their bright colors.

"Whew," snorted Ollie. "It stinks in here."

"Yeah, dead fish are like relatives," said one of the crabs. "They begin to smell if they're around too long."

"Is that a crack about my mom?" asked another crab.

"I wasn't thinking of her, but now that you mention it…"

"You no good micro-algae eater!"

The two crabs began bashing each other with their claws.

Pretty soon all the crabs were fighting, and once again, looked like one, big, tangled mess.

"You know," said Ollie. "If you crabs worked together you could have gotten out of this smelly container by now."

"Who asked you?" snorted one of the crabs, that had a head lock on another.

"Whatever."

The outside shackle to the container rattled and the lid slid back. Bright flood lights from the pier forced Ollie to squint as he looked up. Red Face reached in and grabbed Ollie. This time he wore thick leather gloves and restrained the little otter so as not to get bitten again. Red Face covered Ollie with a towel and the otter's eyes with one of the big mitts.

It seemed to Ollie that Red Face carried him like this over the rickety wharf planks for a long time. Finally Red Face pulled back his gloved hand so that Ollie could see.

"Here he is," commented Red Face. "He's got a cut paw, but he's a perfect specimen, really."

"Oh, he's adorable," said the woman. "Thanks for rescuing this young otter and notifying the Sea Park."

"This ain't charity, Miss," grunted Red Face. "I expect to be paid."

"Paid?"

"A thousand bucks ought to do it."

"That's blackmail! Other fishermen help the otters, expecting nothing in return."

"I ain't other fisherman."

"The Sea Park won't pay bribe money."

"Five hundred. And that's only because I leave town tomorrow."

"I didn't expect this."

"Then you can expect to find a dead otter."

"That's against the law!"

"Catch me if you can," calmly uttered Red Face, as he turned with Ollie and walked away.

"Please stop," said the woman. "The otter is more important to me than the money. But all I've got is my own twenty dollars. I don't get paid until Friday."

"Sorry, that won't cut it," said Red Face, without stopping.

"I have a gold necklace and pearl!"

Red Face stopped. He turned only his mug and sniffed the salty air as if he could breathe in the jewelry's value.

Ollie watched the woman clutch the dangling pearl.

"My father gave this to me before he died."

"Sorry to hear that."

"It hurt me a lot worse than it hurt you, obviously."

"C'mon Miss, you gonna fork it over or not?" asked Red Face, his uncaring eyes canvassing the dock for fish and game wardens.

The woman glanced at Ollie who made a delicate crying noise, uncomfortable in the gruff fisherman's arms. She unclasped the gold necklace with single pearl and gave it to Red Face.

"That's a rare pearl," said the woman.

"And that's a rare otter," replied Red Face, handing her Ollie with calloused hands.

Ollie immediately sensed a difference between the humans as the woman held him closely and caressed his fur.

"Don't you worry about a thing," said the woman. "I'm taking you to a good place."

CHAPTER 5

Bingo the Bird

Ollie didn't like the cold feel of the stainless steel tray he sat on. His paws couldn't grip and the woman gently held him in place.

"Good weight," said the woman. "You're a healthy juvenile."

She carefully wrapped gauze and tape over Ollie's paw, allowing him to lick ice cubes in a bowl.

"Ten stitches. Young and alone in the wild you might not have made it. You're lucky we got you."

She carefully set Ollie into an open cage with fluffy-warm towels and chew toys.

"You're going to love playing with the other otters. We've got two males about your age, Fuzzy and Browner. And a female named Sadie who's as cute as can be."

She fed Ollie abalone trimmings from a bucket. The famished otter eagerly accepted the treats.

"You're a hungry little guy."

A big indigo-blue bird with a black beak perched on a stand nearby. The bizarre yet majestic bird cocked its head and stared at Ollie with yellow-ringed eyes.

Ollie thought that the bird looked nothing like a seagull or pelican.

"You're a hungry little guy," whistled the bird, surprising Ollie. "Make him fat Kris, make him fat. Make him fat Kris, make him fat."

The woman laughed.

"In case you didn't figure it out, my name's Kris," said the woman, formally introducing herself to Ollie, as if he might understand her. "Kris with a K."

"Kris with a K," repeated the bird. "Kris with a K."

"And that's Bingo," said Kris. "He's a hyacinth macaw. When he gets on a roll he repeats everything you say."

"Repeats everything you say," chimed Bingo. "Repeats everything you say."

Kris hand fed Ollie one last piece of abalone.

"You're going to be okay. I love you so much!"

Ollie lifted his chin and bobbed his head as if to say, *thank you*.

"You're welcome," said Kris. "Tonight you're going to sleep in here. Bingo will keep you company. Tomorrow you go outside in the water with your new friends."

Ollie rolled in the fresh cloth as if it were kelp leaves. He felt warm and safe.

Kris smiled and left the room, saying, "See you in the morning."

"See you in the morning," whistled Bingo. "See you in the morning."

The door shut behind Kris.

"See you in the STINKING, SANITIZED, ANOTHER LOUSY DAY-MORNING," ranted Bingo. "Thank Goodness she's gone. Now I can stop that repeating malarkey. The things I gotta do for bird feed."

"Malarkey?" asked Ollie. "My grandpa says that word."

"I'm from the old school, Kid."

"Maybe you should tell her you don't want to repeat words," suggested Ollie.

"Look Kid, this is the Sea Park, alright? Otters and seals do tricks. I gotta do the pirate-bird schtick. It's a living."

"Yeah, but…"

"It'll be my tail feathers if I don't do what they expect. A long time ago some dumb bird started the 'polly wanna cracker' routine and now it's what we exotics gotta do all day long. Sheesh."

"I still say you should talk to her about it," insisted Ollie.

"Talk to her about it? Haven't ya figured it out? We can't talk to people like we can to each other. They're humans. Ya gotta repeat the things they say or move your head around or flap your flippers like the seals do. They don't understand us."

"Oh."

Bingo walked down his perch, jumped onto the table and then to the floor. He waddled over to Ollie.

"So what's your name, Kid?"

"Ollie."

"Ollie the otter," Bingo said with a smirk. "That's original. If it ain't Ollie, it'd have to be Oscar, Ozzie, or Oba-longa-dooie."

"Are you making fun of me?"

"Just 'O' names, Kid," squawked Bingo. "I give everybody a hard time. If people put words in your mouth every day, wouldn't your feathers be ruffled?"

"I guess."

"Look. I'll help ya out. I'll repeat your name a few times and

Kris will get the clue to name you Ollie."

"Thanks. I wouldn't want her calling me something else."

"Like Squid Butt?"

"That's not what I was thinking."

"Where I come from, Kid, my name was Samson. I had more chest feathers and mating calls than any guy macaw in the Amazon valley. Then one day I got doped, sacked, and ended up here. Now Bingo is my name-o."

"Humans are bad," said Ollie.

"Another cliché in the wild, Kid. Kris is nicer than any bird I ever knew. Ya got your mostly good humans and your one or two bad humans. Just do your tricks and you'll be fine."

"What's a trick?"

"It's a gimmick, like the way I repeat words. Seals juggle balls and do silly skits. Otters push basketballs around the pool, do rollovers for fish, and chase each other. Ya got it easy being an otter, really."

"Rollovers for fish?" asked Ollie, looking none too pleased.

"You're not 'out there' anymore, Kid. You're in a human freak-show thing. Ya gotta do a bunch of goofy stuff to make the humans clap and snort and what not. The more they like ya, the more food ya get."

"So they just give you food, like she was doing with me before?"

"Yep. Beats groveling in the wild. But ya get some processed stuff, not as much fiber in your diet. When my gizzard acts up I just fly over the crowd and let 'em have it."

"You can fly?"

"Of course I can! I'm a bird you knuckle dragger!"

"Then why don't you fly home?"

"Home? To South America? Hello! You don't get out much do ya? Could you see me taking up residence in some palm tree with other parrot runaways that preen their feathers for parasites? That ain't my idea of a Tarzan movie!"

"But still, couldn't you..."

"Look, my bird brain can't handle all of your questions," said Bingo, waddling back to his perch. "You're safe here. You'll be well fed. A wild guy like you might get bored. But what the heck, it's a living."

Ollie persisted, "But, wouldn't it be worth it, to try and fly home?"

"Kid, the Sea Park's got its plusses and minuses. Yeah, sometimes I miss the fruits of the Amazon. But here I don't have jaguars on the prowl or Watoobi warriors shooting blow darts at me."

A noticeable regret lingered in Bingo's voice. Ollie clearly heard the stab of remorse. It reminded him to keep vigilant and find his way back to Otter Rock.

"But here's the deal and I'll give it to ya straight," explained Bingo. "You're almost an extinct species."

"What's an extinct feces?" asked Ollie.

"Species not feces. You go around saying feces to people and no one will talk to ya."

"Oh."

"Extinct means 'no more', bye-bye, finished, over, hasta la vista. And species means the kind of animal you are, an otter. What I'm trying to say, is there aren't many more like you, Kid."

"Is that true?"

"Don't test my patience, Bucko. Notice the yellow-ringed eye?"

Bingo pointed a talon to the big peeper.

"Means I don't lie. The message I'm trying to make is that the humans will spoil you rotten, and as soon as that paw of yours is better, they'll turn you loose. This is a rest stop. They want you to go out *there* and make more little otters. Good night and sweet dreams, Kid."

"Thanks Bingo," replied Ollie, feeling relieved but uncertain.

Ollie wondered what the Amazon looked like. *Were there*

abalone and urchins there? Did otters swim by its shores? If so, were they also nearly extinct? He had so many more questions that he wanted to ask Bingo. Before long though, he was fast asleep dreaming of the kelp beds at Otter Rock.

CHAPTER 6

The Sea Park Pool

Ollie could tell it was morning, but he was too comfortable curled up in the bed of towels to even lift his head when the door opened.

"Ollie the otter!" crowed Bingo loudly. "Ollie the otter!"

Kris entered the room and laughed at dark blue macaw.

"Ollie, huh?"

"Ollie the otter!" repeated Bingo. "Ollie the otter!"

"Well little guy, looks like we've got a name for you," said Kris. "I don't know how Bingo does it, but he always seems to come up with perfect names."

"Nod your head, Kid," said Bingo to Ollie.

The little otter vigorously nodded his head and Kris smiled.

"Ollie it is," said Kris.

"Remember that nodding thing, Kid," said Bingo. "It means more abalone strips for ya."

"Can't she hear us?" asked Ollie, stealing a glance towards Kris.

"What? You lived on one rock your whole life? Of course she can't! Like I was saying before, humans are on another wave-length!"

"Oh."

Kris opened Ollie's cage.

"C'mon Ollie. Time to go outside and meet your new friends."

Kris walked to the door and Ollie scampered after her.

"Good luck, Kid," whistled Bingo. "And don't let any of the domestics push ya around."

"You want to come?" asked Kris, looking at Bingo and opening the door for Ollie.

"Out the door," repeated Bingo. "Out the door."

Bingo swooped from his perch, landing next to Ollie.

"You've brought something fresh, something wild, Kid. I feel like a proud bird again."

"You can help me keep an eye on Ollie for his first day with the other animals," Kris said to Bingo.

Bingo flitted up to Kris' shoulder, rubbing his beak with a wing tip. "Kid," said Bingo. "I'll be your coach."

"I don't need a coach."

"Yeah, but you'll have another twenty questions you'll need answers for."

Ollie was more excited than he'd been in a day, and for an otter, that's a long time. Kris opened another door. There before him was a miniature ocean with kelp and several otters floating on their backs, snacking on crab legs.

"It's all yours, Ollie," said Kris. "Go for it!"

"But take it easy," warned Bingo. "The pads on your paws aren't used to the cement, yet!"

Ollie ignored the majestic macaw. Bandaged and all, Ollie took off in a limping mad dash to the pool. He got to the edge and stopped before jumping in. The pads on his forepaws suddenly hurt, especially the one that had been stitched. He noticed that his sensitive paw pads were scraped.

"You're little mitts will get used to the deck in no time," said an old bull seal with a distinct French accent. "Remember, walk don't run."

"Thanks."

"I'm Fandango. They call me out for the big events."

"Oh."

"Listen little otter pup," said Fandango. "I must ask you. Did any girl seals come in with you?"

"Nope. Just me."

Bingo waddled over to the edge of the pool and squawked, "Leave the little guy alone you old flame out!"

The big seal stretched and yawned. Then he bellowed an old bull seal roar and blew Bingo head over talons until the poor bird crashed in a heap near some props. Fandango flapped his flippers together for a finale and barked as if he had just put on a show.

"Little puppy," said Fandango with a French flair. "You must learn to play for the crowd."

"You could have hurt Bingo, you big walrus!" yelled Ollie, knowing seals hated to be called walrus.

"I like an otter that sticks up for his friends," sniffed Fandango, raising an eyebrow. "Most of you are such little kelp fairies, you know."

"Kelp fairies! Humphhh. You're the one who talks different."

"It is my French accent. I am a bull seal from the French Riviera."

"What's French Riviera?"

"It is in France, a country."

"France-schmance!" blurted Bingo who squawked his way towards Ollie. "Fandango's from Spain, can't ya tell by his name? Pierre and Jacques, those are French names."

"You rude little pigeon!" retorted Fandango with his suave intonation. "My first zoo keeper christened me Fandango and she was from Spain! But I bleed French blood!"

Ollie wasn't paying attention to Bingo and Fandango because his vision had met the glance of the prettiest otter he'd ever seen. Never before had he witnessed an otter with blue eyes. Set against dark brown fur, the windows to her soul sparkled like gems. She lifted her head above the waterline for a better peek at Ollie. Ollie's heart thumped in his chest. His throat suddenly became dry and his stomach nervous. He wondered why he felt this way.

"It is the girl, little puppy," crooned Fandango. "She does this to you, her eyes so blue. **She makes your heart sing!**"

"Your head's got a ding," loudly squawked Bingo.

FANDANGO: *The girl does this to you, she makes your heart dance! So, go ahead, hop about and prance!*

OLLIE: *Not a chance.*

FANDANGO: *You may be shy, but give it a try. Her eyes are such a start! Stand up now, and move your feet, feel your beating heart!*

Ollie and the girl otter looked at each other. She smiled, Ollie gulped. Ollie's heart beat so hard he felt as if it had leapt out across the pool and touched hers.

FANDANGO: *Song and dance, I think of France. Come here my sweet daisy!*

BINGO: *This seal's crazy!*

Fandango grabbed Bingo and pulled the bird into a tango dance hold. Dark blue feathers flew in all directions.

FANDANGO: *The more you dance, the more you sing, you will quench your heart's desire! Go ahead, fan the flames, feel your heart's fire! Up-up-up we go, until we touch the sky! Go ahead, dance and sing, let your heart fly!"*

BINGO: *Not I!*

Fandango twirled Bingo upside down, in the air.

FANDANGO: *It is you, it is me, our love so high! Now that our hearts are one, we'll be together until we die!*

BINGO: *I'm gonna cry.*

Ollie's eyes looked dreamy as he stood smitten, near the edge of the pool. The girl otter's eyes twinkled.

FANDANGO: *Let me buy you things and take you places! The tourists watching, oh the faces! Our sweet love and the bliss! The unspoken word, let us kiss!"*

BINGO: *Boo, hiss!*

Fandango bent Bingo over backwards and kissed him.

Bingo spit and wiped off his big black beak, crowing,

"Ughhh!"

Ollie, drunk with love, fell into the pool. The other otters laughed at him. Ollie surfaced, quite embarrassed.

Humans passing by the viewing gallery stopped and clapped, delighted at the animals' spontaneous performance.

"Good job Fandango!" exclaimed Kris, and she tossed him a fish. "It wasn't even show time. You too, Bingo. Are you all right?"

"Are you all right?" mimicked Bingo, tired. "Are you all right?" The bedraggled bird barely caught the fig fruit that Kris tossed.

A bunch of teenagers pointed and laughed at Bingo from the viewing gallery.

"Ya geeks," mumbled Bingo under his breath. "Get a life."

Ollie stared at Sadie over a narrow ribbon of kelp. Sadie seemed equally love struck.

"Ollie, it looks like you've met Sadie," said Kris, and she tossed them each an oyster. Sadie gulped hers down. Like a true otter gentleman, Ollie handed his to her. Sadie's otter lips formed a shy smile as she sighed.

"Get a load of this," said Fuzzy the otter to his brother Browner. "They're goo-goo eyes all over the place."

Fuzzy swiped the oyster from Sadie and gulped it down himself.

"Fuzzy!" warned Kris, "wait for your own food. You too Browner."

Ollie stared at Fuzzy. This domestic little poacher would soon know who'd be boss of the otter pool.

"You want a fat lip?" warned Ollie.

"Oh don't mind them," said Sadie, her voice soft and sweet. "They're my brothers. The one with all the fur is Fuzzy. The other is Brown Nose but we call him Browner."

"Brown Nose?" asked Ollie. "All otters have brown noses."

"He kisses up for food," blurted Fuzzy. "Watch."

Browner scampered out of the pool and followed Kris wherever she went. The little otter didn't take his eyes off the food bucket.

"Browner," said Kris, "I just gave you something to eat." Yet Kris reached into the pail for another morsel. "Okay, here you go. Do a rollover for the kids."

Kris waved an anchovy and Browner performed a rollover. A

group of children in the viewing area laughed and pointed their fingers and clapped. Browner gulped down his treat.

"Pathetic," said Ollie. "You'll never catch me begging. Doing rollovers for *fish*. That's disgusting."

"Maybe not, but you did a flip for *her*," commented Fuzzy.

Sadie splashed water in her brother's face.

"How often does she feed you anchovies?" Ollie spitted, as if just the thought made him sick to his stomach.

"Most of the time," answered Sadie. "For dessert and special days we get invertebrates like abalone and sea urchins."

"I'm gonna die," moaned Ollie. "I'm used to eating abalone and urchins whenever I want. I never have to eat anchovies. Rock cod maybe, but anchovies, no way."

Ollie looked under a kelp leaf and asked, "How about brown turban snails?"

"They sound delicious."

"Where there's kelp, there's brown turbans," said Ollie, as if he was a big-chested adult male that commanded miles of territory. "I'll get you one."

Sadie batted her eyes as she rested on her back in the kelp.

"I'll get one first!" shouted Fuzzy.

"You can't even spell brown turban," scoffed Ollie.

"I may have been born in captivity, but I know every inch of this pool," said Fuzzy. "If there's a snail in here, I'll find it. And I'll get it before you."

"You're on!" yelled Ollie. He turned to Sadie and whispered, "I'll even crack the shell for you, so you don't get slime on your fur."

Sadie twitched her flippers, excited.

Browner counted them down: "ONE. TWO. THREE. GO!"

Ollie flipped his hindflippers and dived. His surface plunge left scarcely a ripple on the water, it was so smooth.

"I'm even gonna let the vagrant have a head start," said Fuzzy, pausing before his dive. "He doesn't stand a chance."

Fuzzy tucked forward, his tail jerked spasmodically, and his flippers thrashed the surface of the tranquil pool.

"The little wild otter, Ollie, showed style and grace in his entrance," commented Fandango. "The spoiled puppy, Fuzzy, he is not French, that is for sure."

Underwater, Ollie propelled himself with hindflipper bicycle kicks. Ollie was used to the ocean's crashing waves, rough surf, and strong currents. Swimming in this placid pool was effortless for him.

Ollie searched up and down the kelp stalks and glanced under the leaves. He had never seen such weak and wimpy kelp. It wasn't as thick or strong as the kelp at Otter Rock. The leaves snapped off much too easily. No turban snails anywhere, either. At Otter Rock, there would have been dozens of brown turbans on each kelp stalk.

Fuzzy's dumb to look for brown turban snails at the bottom of the pool, thought Ollie.

Ollie saw Fuzzy grab an object and shoot to the surface. Curious, Ollie followed him. Fuzzy rolled onto his back and placed a big squeaky toy, rubber snail, on his tummy.

"That's not a real one," said Ollie.

"So!" sassed Fuzzy. "I got a snail, first, didn't I? Bet's a bet."

"Watch and learn spoiled boy," said Ollie, as he bolted under the water.

It seemed like a long time passed as Ollie searched everywhere for a real brown turban snail. He was used to diving to a hundred feet deep in the ocean, and holding his breath up to three minutes. Sadie, Fuzzy, and Browner grew up in only ten feet of water, so their lungs weren't as developed.

"This guy can sure hold his breath," admitted Fuzzy.

"Yeah, he's been down twice as long as we could have been," said Browner.

"Wow," murmured Sadie, impressed.

Fuzzy and Browner looked at each other, making exaggerated goo-goo faces. Fuzzy imitated Sadie, saying, "Wow."

"Wow," repeated Browner, as syrupy as he could.

The two brothers kept saying, "Wow", back and forth, teasing Sadie, until she nipped at them. Only then did they stop.

Ollie surfaced quietly, his head down.

"Did you find one?" asked Sadie.

"Nope," said Ollie. "And I looked under every kelp leaf and down every stalk."

"Look out!" shouted Fuzzy. "Cannon ball!"

Up on the slide platform, Ironhead the giant sea turtle had tucked his arms, legs, and head inside his shell, and teetered on the ledge. Ironhead was about to make a monster splash.

Before the otters could react, Ironhead hit the drink with three hundred pounds of full impact. A column of water shot skyward. A turtle Tsunami rocked within the pool, making a wave that launched Fuzzy up onto the deck. Kris, Fandango, and Bingo all got soaked. Even some of the humans on the gallery platform got wet. Ironhead slowly surfaced with a big, stupid smile on his face.

"Gee, hope I didn't scare the new fella."

Sadie and Browner swallowed some water and coughed. Ollie rolled up and down in the waves, loving it.

"Do it again!" exclaimed Ollie.

"Okay Ironhead," said Kris, not sounding too happy. "If you're that bored, it's time for you to earn your keep."

"Ahh darn," moaned Ironhead. "I was just trying to have some fun."

"Over here otters," said Kris, tapping the food bucket. "Who wants to ride the turtle's back?"

Sadie and Browner swam to the edge of the pool. Fuzzy snaked his way over from the far side of the deck.

"Come here Ironhead," said Kris.

The big sea turtle stroked with his flippers until he nudged his head to the pool's trough.

"This is all I'm good for," said Ironhead, feeling sorry for him-self. "A boat ride."

Kris dropped a specially made harness over the sea turtle's head and pulled two of his big leathery flippers through. A rope and handle draped over Ironhead's back.

"You first, Fuzzy," said Kris. "Show Ollie how it's done."

Ollie continued floating on his back in the kelp canopy, feeling comfortable.

"Come here Ollie," said Kris, tapping the food pail. "Will you come out with the others?"

Ollie ignored her, rolling up in a kelp blanket instead.

"Okay, have it your way," said Kris as she tossed him a whole squid.

Meanwhile, Fuzzy had climbed onto Ironhead's back and grabbed the rope's handle with his paws. The turtle looked back, saw that Fuzzy was ready, and began swimming.

This looks like fun, thought Ollie.

He swam over and tried to climb aboard, but couldn't because Ironhead's shell was too slippery and he had only one good paw. So Ollie grabbed hold of a kelp stalk, bit it in half, and approached the big sea turtle again. Ollie felt his hurt paw but forgot the pain when fun was involved.

Ollie tied one end of the stalk to the harness, held onto the other, and let himself be towed. Then Ollie used the kelp rope to hoist himself aboard Ironhead's back.

While Fuzzy sat on Ironhead's shell, Ollie stood up, and held the kelp rope with his good paw, turtle skiing. After one lap around the small pool, Ollie even lifted a hindflipper, showing off. Then he wrapped the kelp around one of his webbed feet and stood atop Ironhead in an acrobatic foreleg stand.

Humans in the galley laughed and pointed and clapped.

"Unbelievable," said Fandango. "Not even a French otter could do that."

"There are no otters in France," squawked Bingo. "In fact, I don't even think there are seals in France or Spain. You're a total act, blubber butt!"

Fandango chased after Bingo who easily flew out of reach.

"Vive la France, you dirty feather duster!" yelled Fandango.

Kris blew a whistle and Ironhead docked. Ollie and Fuzzy jumped off. Kris reached into her food bucket and tossed Ironhead a couple of fish. She reached into a separate pouch and retrieved a wriggling gob of fat innkeeper worms for all the otters.

Fuzzy and Browner stood upright, begging for the juicy, but ugly worms. Kris gave them each a handful, which they slurped down like spaghetti noodles.

"Fish is one thing, but innkeeper worms?" retorted Ollie. "No otter I know stooped so low to eat innkeeper worms."

"I won't eat them if you won't," said Sadie, showing support.

"Here you go," said Kris, handing a mess of worms to Sadie.

But the little otter turned away.

"Sadie?" asked Kris. "What's with you?"

Kris tried to offer the worms to Ollie who looked like he couldn't be bothered with such drool.

"Oh, now I get it," said Kris. "Because Ollie doesn't like innkeeper worms, now you don't either." Kris thought for a moment, then added, "Ollie learned to like certain foods because that's what his mother brought him when he was a pup. But Sadie, you learned to like other foods."

Kris pulled some anchovies out of the shiny pail. Sadie was tempted, and hungry, but she declined the offering.

"You learned that behavior quickly," said Kris, trying to figure this situation out.

Kris gave the fish to Ironhead, Fuzzy, and Brown Nose, who gobbled eagerly. Even Fandango got into the act, slapping his flippers together and barking so that he might get some. Kris fed all the animals, except for Ollie and Sadie.

Kris squatted down to the eye level of the hold-out otters.

"I'll go get some squid for you two rebels. But starting tomorrow, Sadie, I hope you'll learn to like fish again. Ollie's okay because he's on the Release Program. As soon as his paw heals, he goes over *there* and eats what he catches for himself. Then we let him go, back to the wild."

Kris left for the squid. Ollie gulped as it hit him like a whale tail on the side of the head: *over there? Behind that fence? AWAY FROM SADIE?*

Both of the otters looked at the chest high fence that surrounded the smaller pool, which seemed far away.

"Otters that go over there don't come back," demurred Sadie.

"Bingo! Coach!" shouted Ollie.

Bingo swooped over with a few wing thrusts, happy to be needed.

"Yo! Coach-Daddy is here!"

"What's that place, there?" asked Ollie, pointing his bandaged paw.

Bingo saw the forlorn look on the two otter's faces and gazed off, into the distance, sighing heavily.

"It's agony and ecstasy. It's a tale of two star crossed lovers, it's yin and yang…"

"Will you stop it?!" said Ollie impatiently."I don't even know what you mean."

Bingo looked squarely at Ollie and said, "It's *The Pen*. That's where otters are put, away from human interaction and the *Lifers*, to get 'em ready for return to the wild."

Ollie's eyes grew bigger at the notion of returning home. But he had to ask, "Lifers?"

"Sadie and her brothers are Lifers. They're not ever going to leave Sea Park. That's the agony part, Kid. Like I was saying."

"But why can't they leave Sea Park with me?" asked Ollie.

"Would you excuse us for a moment?" Bingo asked Sadie, while nesting a protective wing over Ollie's shoulder.

Sadie nodded her head and slid backwards into the water. Bingo stepped away from the pool, guiding Ollie.

"Sadie and her brothers were triplets. That's rare for otters. Something bad happened to their mom and they ended up here, when they were little. They were so tiny, that Kris and the other humans had to feed 'em fish formula-glop from an eye dropper."

Bingo held up one talon, as if to demonstrate the small size of the baby otters.

"They were like only this big. Cutest little-furry-poop machines ya ever saw."

Bingo took his wing off Ollie's shoulder, squarely facing the otter.

"The humans worked day and night to keep the little runts alive," continued Bingo. "When they got bigger, Kris and the other trainers took 'em on swim excursions, the whole bit. Tried to get 'em comfortable in the wild. Made me want to puke. Did I ever get the coddling treatment? Anyway, it never worked out for Sadie and her brothers to adapt to the wild, no matter how much the humans tried. That's why they're *Lifers*. Get past your love for her, Kid. It's over."

CHAPTER 7

Ollie's Nightmare

Kris had fed Ollie his fill of squid, and Sadie and her brothers nestled closely to him in a mound of blankets, sleeping. Ollie tossed and turned, occasionally stealing a peek at Sadie. He kept hearing Bingo's words play over and over again in his head: "Get past your love for her, Kid. It's over."

Sadie looked so cute as she slept, he thought. Finally, after most of the night had gone by, he too fell asleep.

Ollie dreamt of Otter Rock. He was back in the lush kelp, frolicking and eating his favorite foods. Sadie was there, Browner and Fuzzy, too.

His happy dream transformed into a terrible nightmare. He was stranded on the Sea Park deck, high up on a prop. He was somehow stuck there and none of the other animals could help him, not even Sadie. Humans booed at him from the gallery. Kris had a black beard and red face. She forced open Ollie's jaws and stuffed innkeeper worms and anchovies into his mouth while shouting, "Eat these ya little water rat!"

Ollie woke up, panting in short bursts. The first thing he noticed was *The Pen.* The deck lights cast an ominous glow on this fenced-in environment. His heart raced. Frightened, he reminded himself that *The Pen* was a good thing, a safe place to get him ready for his return to Otter Rock.

The Pen seemed to change before his eyes. It no longer looked like a horror-pool or anything scary like that. Just a place. In fact, it looked fun to Ollie, now that he looked at it with a positive frame of mind. It featured a big pipe that spouted sparkling water into a pool. This torrent of ocean spray looked exciting.

Ollie looked around the Sea Park deck. All of the animals were asleep, including Bingo, Ironhead, and Fandango. Sadie had a sweet smile on her face. There was no torture prop like he'd seen in his dream. Ollie stared at the ten foot wall that kept them enclosed, separated from the real beach and ocean. The night was silent except for the sound of the ocean waves, just beyond the Sea Park enclosure.

Ollie sniffed the air and smelled the fresh sea aroma. He licked at the sky and tasted the sting of salt. Ollie remembered his vow on the boat, to once again see his mom and dad. He recalled the sorrowful tone in Bingo's voice as the bird had talked about being stolen from his home in the Amazon Valley. Ollie was glad that he would be returning to where he belonged.

He looked down at Sadie. He realized he loved her more than any otter he'd ever met, except for maybe his parents. Ollie decided he'd like her to be his mate. They might someday have their own otter pup. But he knew that he would be leaving Sadie, forever. The forever feeling hurt him, on the inside, just as much as being away from his home.

Ollie knew he had to go back to Otter Rock, but he didn't want to leave Sadie. This was going to be a problem.

CHAPTER 8

The Operation

Weeks passed and Ollie's paw mended perfectly.

"Looks good, don't you think?" said Kris, examining his paw.

"Very nice," said Sasha, another animal trainer. "He's ready. Tomorrow Ollie gets to catch food by himself. But today, he gets his radio transmitter."

Sasha wore brightly colored hair ties that Ollie often pulled loose from her matted hair. Ollie enjoyed Sasha's long dredlocks that dangled like ropes. He liked tugging on them.

"While we're waiting for the Doctor, show Sasha the trick we've been working on," said Kris.

Kris grabbed hold of Ollie's rear end.

"Pull your tail up to your chest, like this, and then flip it down, hard."

Ollie refused to flip his tail down. Instead, he rolled over onto his back and looked at her with an innocent face.

"Ollie, all the other otters can do it."

Browner and Fuzzy had been watching and immediately each did a front-tuck flip.

"They're teasing you," laughed Sasha. "But Ollie's resistance is a good sign. He's ready to be on his own."

"I bet he could do ten front-tucks if he wanted," said Kris.

"I doubt it," said the more experienced Sasha. "It's not something I've seen them do in the wild."

Ollie scampered over to a bunch of towels and hid underneath them while the other otters did front-tuck flips in the water. The human viewers up in the galley section began clapping and cheering.

"Look at all the people that came," said Kris. "They're hoping Ollie will ride Ironhead."

"C'mon Ollie," beckoned Sasha. "Show the people your stuff."

But Ollie whimpered and stayed under the towels.

"Do some front-tucks with us, Ollie," pleaded Fuzzy and Browner. "They'll feed ya fish!"

"They're tasty, in a salty kind of way," added Sadie.

But Ollie didn't care about doing any "worthless" front-tuck flips, especially for fish. Bingo flew from his perch, closer to Ollie, and woke up Fandango who had been asleep in the sun.

"I'm worried about ya, Kid," said Bingo. "You're not even playing with Sadie anymore."

"Why should I? I gotta go and she has to stay."

"Enjoy yourself, little elf, while you can. Besides, you love her," said Fandango.

"Don't remind me," said Ollie, covering his head with a towel.

"Yes-yes little Ollie," crooned Fandango. "She is a beautiful otter-girl."

"I don't want to think about it," squeaked Ollie.

"Then think about *this*, the humans are going to operate on you in an hour," stabbed Bingo.

"Maybe you could have said that in another way?" asked Fandango.

"Another way, another schmay," said Bingo. "Time's running out for Ollie, here."

By now Ollie had learned Bingo's way. It was usually better to have him tell you everything in one burst, no matter how painful.

"Okay Bingo. Give it to me, I can take it."

Bingo took a deep breath and let it rip, "They're going to take you into another room and make you breathe some stuff. You'll go 'night-night' real fast. A human they call the Doctor, with a sharp knife and a funny hat, will cut a slice into your gut, which they call 'the abdominal cavity'. He'll shove in a little beepy-gizmo thing, a radio transmitter."

"The transmitter does not hurt, though," interrupted Fandango, patting a flipper on his stomach. "I have one, but the battery died a long time ago."

"I've got the floor, Lard Lips, don't cut in," said Bingo. "So this transmitter allows them to track you when you're released. Spy situation. They'll give you a week in the other pool, start you swimming in the ocean, then you take off to the wild blue yonder one day, and that's it. See ya, wouldn't wanna be ya."

An otter paw pulled back Ollie's towel.

"Will you come play, Ollie," asked Sadie. "I saved my abalone strip for you."

"You're a dominant otter, Kid," said Bingo. "As an adult, you'll probably command a large territory. You're not the type to do front-tuck flips for fish."

"Yes, but didn't I say he was a French otter?" said Fandango. "Look at him, he is in love."

Ollie was transfixed on Sadie. In that moment he knew he could not leave her. That was it, she had to come with him. But would she? And how?

CHAPTER 9

Agenda of the Animals

Some time after Ollie's minor operation to implant the radio transmitter, he was alone in his pen. There was a bright orange identification tag now fixed to one of his hindflippers. It upset him to see his friends on the other side of the fence, especially Sadie, and not even be able to play with them. But Ollie got to crack his own crabs and he had a plan.

Ollie peered through the fence as Kris and Sasha said their normal 'good nights' to each animal.

When Kris stopped to see Ollie, he playfully pulled on her hair, which he'd never done before.

"What's gotten into you, Ollie?"

Ollie licked under her chin and Kris felt for the pearl necklace that was no longer there.

"You make me remember my dad with your licks. I used to wear a necklace that he gave me. You're that necklace now."

Ollie pressed his head against her heart. Kris was quite surprised and touched. No otter had muzzled her so directly before.

"This is the last time I can touch you, Ollie."

Ollie also batted Sasha's dredlocks around, refusing to let go of one exceptionally long clump-strand of hair.

"Hey," said Sasha, "And this is the last time you can play with my dreds. No more human contact. It's for your own good."

But Ollie wouldn't let go. Kris had to help Sasha by gently pulling Ollie's paws loose. Finally, Kris and Sasha left the deck and shut the door behind themselves.

"Coach!" yelled Ollie. "Time for Mission Fat-Fish!"

"Mission what?" asked Bingo, flying over with a rope hanging from his beak. "It's gotta be Code-Red or Bravo-Louie, something *macho*. Mission Fat-Fish? Sheesh."

"Macho?" questioned Ollie.

"I don't do Spanish lessons, Kid."

Bingo kept one rope end in his beak and threw the other to

Ollie. Ollie quickly climbed the fence and scurried over to his surprised friends.

"I'm so happy to see you!" blurted Sadie.

"Me too," said Browner.

"Me three," said Fuzzy.

"Yeah, things were getting pretty boring without you around," said Ironhead.

"I have a plan," stated Ollie. "It's Mission Code-Louie."

"Code-Red or Bravo-Louie, not Code-Louie!" squawked Bingo.

"Whatever," said Ollie. "I'm leaving Sea Park and I want you to all come with me."

Fandango's lower jaw nearly hit the cement deck. Sadie got excited for an instant, then realized the magnitude of what Ollie had asked. Fuzzy and Browner didn't think it made any sense at all.

"Would we be back in time for lunch?" asked Ironhead, not getting it. "I like lunch a lot."

"No, Ironhead. I mean to leave Sea Park for good. To swim and live in the ocean with all the wild otters and sea turtles."

"What for?" asked Ironhead.

"Because, well, life is, oh gosh, it's a long story," answered Ollie, figuring it might best for Ironhead to stay at Sea Park.

"I'll go," volunteered Sadie.

"Thank the Deep Blue Sea!" yelled Ollie, not shy about expressing his excitement. "I hoped you would."

Sadie blushed.

"What about us?" asked Fuzzy. "I don't want to leave Sea Park. Neither does Brown Nose, do you Browner?"

"No way," said Browner. "I've heard stories about life on the outside. Sounds glamorous, but scary too. We've got it made here, why leave?"

"How about you?" Fuzzy asked Bingo. "You're a smart bird."

"I'm flying the coop, Kid," whistled Bingo, his yellow-ringed eyes growing big. "I need to spread my wings and meet a few chicks."

Fuzzy turned to the French seal, who still looked shocked by the whole thing.

"Fandango?"

"I am flabbergasted. I am, how you say, discombobulated."

"Would you use smaller words, please," requested Browner.

"Yeah, does it mean you're staying or going?" asked Fuzzy.

"I think it means he has to use the bathroom," squawked Bingo.

"It means that I'm not sure!" blurted Fandango. "I like the idea of the adventure, the women seals I might meet, but the ocean can be a rough place!"

"Great white sharks," chimed Fuzzy with fear and awe. "I've seen pictures of those beasts. The teeth, the eyes that roll back when they bite. Forget it!"

"And oil spills," said Fandango. "Remember, that's what brought me here when I was a pup. I get sick to my stomach just thinking of that black goo!"

"And fishermen might hurt us!" added Fuzzy. "That's why Ollie's here!"

"And having to forage for food all the time?" questioned Browner. "Geez, I put away twenty pounds of fish a day. Can you imagine having to work for all that grub?"

"It's easy and fun," said Ollie. "Instead of picking up rubber squeaky toys, you get the real thing. You get what you want instead of settling for anchovies. The feeling of being on your own and depending on others, like hunting for food and protecting one another, makes you feel *alive*. We're all just going through the motions here. I gotta bust loose."

"Stay," pleaded Browner. "I'll save up all my invertebrates for you."

"Yeah," added Fuzzy. "So will I. You'll never miss a meal."

"They're gonna return him to the wild anyway," said Bingo.

"Thanks guys, really," said Ollie. "What I'm talking about is *that* feeling. How you offered to give me something that means a lot to you. In the wild, living with others that depend on you, you get that feeling every day."

Ollie watched Browner and Fuzzy's eyes grow big, even though they gulped air nervously. He knew that in that moment, they had felt the good feeling of giving and understood what he meant.

Ollie scurried to the water's edge and grabbed some kelp. He raced back to the group. He held the kelp up for all to see.

"See this stuff?"

They all looked at it. Ollie tried to pop the kelp bulb, but it only flattened out, limpid.

"Out there, this thing would have popped with fresh juice. You could bite into it and taste the sweet nectar. The kelp bakes in the sun all day, soaking in the sun's rays. When you eat it fresh, you eat those sunbeams."

The animals' faces were riveted on Ollie, his speech contagious. Ollie sensed the building momentum and went into overdrive.

"You can then dive to a hundred feet in the water and hold your breath for a long time and even *stand up* on a turtle's back if you want. This stuff here has been dead for a month!"

Ollie paused, making eye contact with each one of them.

"Everything here is like that, including all of you."

Ollie saw that his words hurt Ironhead. He didn't want the sensitive turtle to think less of himself.

"I'm sorry, Ironhead. Maybe I exaggerated."

"No, you didn't," said the sea turtle. "I remember seeing plankton sparkles in the ocean at night. If you swam into a cluster of sparkles, you felt tingles. I don't tingle here. I want to tingle, again."

"What about great white sharks?" asked Fuzzy.

"All you gotta do is stay in the kelp," said Ollie.

"And oil spills?" asked Fandango.

"That's out of our control," replied Ollie. "But then if one of the trainers doesn't show up for a meal, you don't eat."

"But that's never happened," said Browner. "Kris and Sasha always take care of us."

"Yeah, but you never know. It's out of our control. And what if Sea Park ships you off to some other aquarium, like that one in New York that Fandango talks about?"

"Not that jungle!" shouted Bingo.

"Don't even think about it!" said Fandango. "You'd be in that animal pit with penguins and walruses!"

"Penguins can't even fly for crying out loud," whistled Bingo, flapping his wings. "And what was mother nature thinking when she dressed 'em in those little black and white tuxedos? Sheesh."

Fuzzy and Browner stood alone in their comfort zone. Ollie looked at them earnestly.

"But don't feel like you have to join us."

The two otters gulped for air, like dying cod on the deck of a boat.

"You know, Browner," said Fuzzy. "Staying here we'd have the run of the place."

"Yeah we would," answered Browner. "We'd have it all to ourselves."

"Yep, all to ourselves."

"No one to bug us."

"More food than ever."

"No doubt about it."

The two brothers looked at each other and realized they could no longer keep up with their false bravado.

CHAPTER 10

Escape from Sea Park

The sun had just peeked over the horizon as Fandango turned the door knob with his flippers. He opened the door from the deck area to the otter infirmary. Fuzzy and Browner were the first to leave their outside refuge, then Sadie, Bingo, Ironhead, and Ollie.

Inside, they crossed by the scale on which Ollie was weighed upon entering Sea Park.

"Wait just a sec," said Bingo. "Let me get a last bite of bird feed."

Bingo waddled to his perch and pecked some sunflower seeds from a feed dish. Fandango opened the door from the otter hospital to the Sea Park museum hallway. The big seal peeked out, then glanced back at his friends. "The coast's clear. Hurry, before any humans come."

One by one they entered the hallway. It was a strange world to them; photographs and real-life exhibits of otters and seals and animals that looked real but didn't move, as if they were frozen stiff.

"They're stuffed," whispered Bingo.

"Stuffed?" asked Ironhead, scared.

"Yeah," said Bingo, quietly. "Something happened to 'em and they got fixed to stay like that. Humans call it a display."

"A display?" asked Sadie.

"Doesn't look like much fun to me," said Ironhead.

"Not play, dis-play," whispered Bingo. "The human kids stand there for hours, just staring at the dead things. Can you believe it?"

"How morbid," said Fandango.

The otters and others scampered, scuttled, and wobbled across the squeaky linoleum. Fandango suddenly froze as he heard a human singing, just around the corner.

"Hurry it up," ushered Fandango, as he reached the exit door and quickly opened it to the outside world.

The singing human was getting closer.

Bingo flew through the door opening and Fandango waved his flipper vigorously, as if that would help the otters and Ironhead to move faster. Sadie made it outside and so did Fuzzy and Browner. Ollie ran back to Ironhead and pushed forcefully on the turtle's shell, to get him moving.

A large bucket of water on wheels suddenly slid into their hallway from the adjoining corridor. The human who was singing loudly was cleaning the floors. He was a short, chubby man, and sloshed a mop across the floor as he worked his way toward the exit door.

Ollie shoved and shoved on the big turtle. If the man turned around, he would see them making their getaway.

Fandango helped Ollie push and the giant sea turtle slid across the shiny floor. Ironhead finally made it through the doorway and Fandango was right behind him.The door shut. The man heard something and turned around, but nothing was there.

The gang of runaway animals stood outside at the top of a long, steep stairway that led to tide pools and the ocean.

"Where's Ollie?" shouted Sadie.

"He must still be inside!" blurted Bingo.

Fandango leaned up against the door and looked back at Bingo. "Flit onto my head and look for him!"

Bingo flapped onto the seal perch and stuck his beak up to the door's thick window, looking all around.

"I can't see Ollie!"

"But he must be there, you stupid bird," said Fandango.

"Knock it off with the stupid or I'll pick your nose with a talon!"

Bingo's yellow-ringed eyes spied Ollie. The smart little otter was standing on his hindflippers, stiff as a board, pretending to be one of the several stuffed otters on display.

"That otter's got brains, I tell ya," said Bingo. "Now crack the door and let me in, Fandangbutt."

"What can you do, fowl mouth?" asked Fandango.

"Don't make me regurgitate my plan," said Bingo.

"Just open the door, slowly. When you hear the man walk away, open it wider for Ollie. Got it?"

"Got it," replied Fandango, gently opening the door.

Bingo squeezed inside and flew as quietly as he could over the man's head and around the corner. The man stopped mopping and looked around, but no one was there. He shrugged his shoulders and continued to sing and slosh his mop around the floor.

"Missed a spot big boy, missed a spot," said Bingo from around the corner. "Missed a spot big boy, missed a spot."

The man stopped mopping.

"That you Kris?"

"Don't quit your day job. Don't quit your day job."

"Okay, Kris, now you know my dream," said the man, walking in the direction of Bingo. "To be a country and western singer."

As the janitor turned the corner, Bingo flew into the air and startled him.

"Ahhh!" blurted the man.

Bingo sailed around the corner and the janitor wheeled around, hiked up his pants, and chased after the feathered escapee, yelling, "Hey!"

But Bingo flew out the door.

CHAPTER 11

The Descent

"Breathe in that salt air and feel the wind!" said Ollie from the top of the stairs. "Don't you feel alive?"

"The human's coming!" warned Bingo as he hovered near the window.

Fandango leaned against the door with all of this might to keep it shut.

"Quick! Down the stairs!"

Ollie and Sadie pushed the rear of Ironhead's shell while Browner and Fuzzy pulled the front. Step by step, they hurried their way down the stairs. Bingo flew and landed, well ahead of the others. The macaw dug his talons into the sand.

"Ahhh, soft, sweet, terra firma."

"Terra what?" quipped Sadie, as she turned around to get her footing on the step below.

"Sand, my little otterette. In fact, I think I'll fill my beak with some."

"Why?" asked Sadie.

"Because I'm a bird and it helps the digestion."

Meanwhile, the janitor forced the door open and the barking Fandango backed off. The janitor kept his distance from the defiant bull seal as Fandango made sure that his friends reached the bottom of the stairs.

Ollie and Sadie jumped to the sand.

"Okay," directed Ollie. "On the count of three, Ironhead comes off the last step. One. Two. Three!"

They pushed and pulled at the same time. Ironhead hit the sand with a thud and a turtle *ooomphhh*.

"The last time I remember being in sand," said Ironhead excitedly, "I broke out from an egg and headed towards the water!"

"You're not the only one who had to hatch," squawked Bingo.

"Bingo!" commanded Ollie. "Go help Fandango!"

"Okay-okay already," chirped Bingo, spitting sand from his

beak. "Doesn't a bird ever get a break?"

Bingo flew to the top of the stairs and flapped and squawked at the janitor. Fandango turned around and shuffled his flippers as fast as he could to get down the stairs. As the janitor came after Fandango, waving his mop, Bingo dive bombed him.

"Hey," yelled the man. "Back off!"

"Back off," mimicked Bingo. "Back off!"

With Bingo's help, Fandango made it to the bottom of the stairs and scurried to the water's edge where the others were waiting.

"They will not gloat, they will come in a boat!" sang Fandango, feeling grand and romantic in the free air.

"And boats go fast," interjected Ollie. "So, we gotta swim as far as we can before hauling ashore. Let's go!"

The animals ventured into the surf except for Ollie.

"C'mon Bingo!" yelled the otter.

Bingo stopped harassing the poor janitor and flew over Ollie's head. Only then did Ollie make his way into the churning ocean.

The janitor scrambled down the steps. He jumped off the bottom stoop and fell in the sand, face first.

Ollie quickly caught up with the others as they approached the large, crashing waves.

"What about great white sharks?" asked Fuzzy.

"They're out further, past the patches of kelp!" shouted Ollie. "They don't like the kelp because their big bodies can get tangled. They might drown. C'mon, let's go!"

CHAPTER 12

The Ocean Swim

Bingo flew high above his friends and watched them swim through the churning whitewash and amidst the pounding waves. Fandango was the most powerful swimmer of the group, even though he was middle aged and out of shape.

Fandango had large front flippers and a strong tail. The otter's little rigid forepaws weren't much help for swimming. They had to depend solely on their webbed hindflippers for thrust. Ironhead's flippers gave him momentum, but his large shelled body was cumbersome to maneuver through the pounding breakers.

Browner, Fuzzy, and Sadie had the hardest time getting

through the surf. A set of big waves caught them and rolled all three domestic otters over and over. Their flippers were tossed into the air, and their heads were pushed under the water. They couldn't breathe. One after another, the waves crashed on top of the three otters, holding them down. Sadie snatched a ribbon of kelp, tearing it loose from the bottom.

Browner pushed with his flippers, pawing at the water, but another wave knocked him back under. Fuzzy pushed off the bottom with a thrust from his hindflippers and reached the surface, where he could finally breathe, only to be pummeled by a wave.

Ollie, Fandango, and Ironhead had burst through the swells. They turned and looked, hoping to see the bobbing heads of their friends.

"Uh-oh," said Ollie. "They must be caught in the whitewash. Swim along the bottom and find them!"

The three little otters were nearly out of air as they were continuously smashed back under the water by crashing waves.

Thankfully Ironhead came to Browner's rescue.

"Hang onto my neck and I'll swim you through!"

Ollie helped Sadie get some air by timing a wave and pushing her to the surface. Ollie guided her along the bottom, under the waves, and past the break line.

Fandango grabbed Fuzzy by the nape of the neck with his mouth.

"Nice and steady because now I'm ready!" barked Fandango, who powered right through the oncoming waves and held Fuzzy securely with his teeth.

"You okay?" asked Ironhead.

"Sort of," answered the beleaguered Browner. "I must have swallowed a gallon of water."

Ollie was able to escort Sadie past the breakers and to the surface.

"Next time, dive under the waves," coached Ollie. "Because you lifted your head up, the wave caught you, slammed you backwards, and then held you down."

"No kidding," coughed Sadie.

"Watch the neck, will ya?" complained Fuzzy as Fandango let him go.

"Would you rather I had let you drown, little clown?" asked Fandango.

"I'd rather you not gouge the back of my neck next time," answered Fuzzy.

Bingo flew down to his friends and hovered, but got sent for a loop in a gust of wind.

"Whoa," said Bingo. "That breeze nearly dropped me in the

drink. I'm going to have to get up high so I can glide."

Bingo flapped his wings and gained altitude. The wind blew hard across the water. Tiny whitecaps formed on the water's surface.

"How we all doing?" asked Ollie.

"Okay," said Sadie.

"Me too," said Browner.

"Me three, sort of," added Fuzzy, as he rubbed the back of his neck.

Fandango rolled around in the water, feeling the great expanse of an ocean without walls. Ironhead lifted his head up, breathing deep of the fresh air.

The janitor jumped up and down on the beach.

"Hey! Come back!"

Finally the man turned and hobbled towards the stairs.

"We better get moving," said Ollie.

The otters swam on their backs with alternating kicks from their hindflippers. Fandango gracefully slid on his belly near the water's surface. Ironhead trudged along, slower than the rest. As they swam, Ollie would occasionally roll over onto his stomach, and swim far ahead. Fandango would join him. Together they hunted for food and by the time the others caught up, Ollie and Fandango had meals for everyone. Even for Bingo.

Ollie got bird food for Bingo by diving to the bottom and grabbing as much sea grass as he could. When he popped to the surface, he spread the delicate green sea weed on Ironhead's back like a salad bar. Bingo would land atop the moving turtle and pick out sea bugs and seed floats from the rich grass.

Sadie liked to pick some of the tiny crabs from the sea grass and eat them, too. They were so different tasting and she could swallow them whole without having to crack the shells.

Ollie taught the otters how to pry the strong muscled abalone from rocks. The biggest challenge in foraging for abalone, the otters learned, was patience and the ability to hold their breath for a long time. The otters banged the tough and hard abalone shells with rocks, to crack the shell and weaken the muscle. Then they had to pull and pull until the abalone came loose.

Up on the surface, they floated on their backs and picked at the soft, white meat. After eating the abalone, they cleaned themselves by twisting and turning in the water. Then they combed their fur until it was dry.

They traveled far down the coast somewhere past Crystal Cove. They'd been fortunate that the Sea Park people hadn't discovered them. At one point, Bingo said he thought he'd seen Kris and Sasha on a boat, but it veered north of Sea Park, closer to the

Crystal Cove pier.

It wouldn't be long now before it got dark. Otters usually stayed in the water at night, sleeping in the kelp. But Ollie knew his domestic otter friends weren't used to that. Only Ironhead would be comfortable staying in the ocean to sleep. They all agreed to push on and haul ashore at the first suitable beach.

CHAPTER 13

To Have Loved and Lost

The Sea Park boat idled near the pilings of the Crystal Cove pier as Kris and Sasha called out the names of the animals:

"Fandango? Ollie? Sadie? Fuzzy? Browner?"

Sasha carefully steadied the radio antennae at the front of the boat and into the darkness before them. Another otter caretaker, Jim, listened for radio transmitter signals and finally uttered, "Nothing."

"But if Ollie's diving underwater, we won't get his signal," said Kris, over the sound of waves crashing up against the pier pilings. "They could still be here."

Again and again they cried out the names until Sasha stopped and sat down, having given up for the time being. Kris kept calling out and looking.

"Maybe we should head south tomorrow morning," said Jim.

"They could also be on the other side of the pier, by the fishing boats," replied Kris, her voice cracking with concern.

"It's dark," Jim tried to reason. "Let's come back in the morning at first light. We can also search with a plane."

"We have to keep looking," blurted Kris.

"I know how badly you want to find them, but it would be better to get a good night's sleep," suggested Sasha.

"But they won't make it if we don't find them."

"We'll find them."

"We'll only find them if we keep looking, tonight!"

"There's only so much we can do," said Sasha.

"I prepared a dozen teenage otters for the wild, once, only to find them dead within two days," confessed Kris. "I can't let that happen again."

Kris felt her throat tighten. She reached for the pearl necklace that she forgot was gone and said, "Every time I love something it seems like I lose it."

CHAPTER 14

Seal Beach

The wayfaring animals swam through the stiff current and around a rocky point. Not much further ahead lay a strip of narrow beach. A group of sea lions barked on the sandy shore.

"I give thanks to the Deep Blue Sea," bellowed Fandango. "Have you ever seen such a beautiful sight? We picked a good spot to spend the night!"

"Hopefully they won't mind if we haul up on their beach," replied Ollie. "Some seals can be pretty territorial, you know."

"I will talk to them, one seal to another," exclaimed Fandango, flapping his strong tail and zipping towards the shore.

Fandango took a small wave and rode it onto the beach. There must have been a dozen seals there, barking to each other, their heads dipping into a crusted aluminum dingy that was partially buried in the sand.

Fandango was greeted by a gruff male who didn't seem to like the French seal encroaching on his turf. This local seal was also quite drunk and dropped his abalone shell, from which sloshed a brown fluid.

"Who are ya and whaddaya want?"

"My name is Fandango. I'm travelling with my friendship band and ask that you let us stay the night on your soft sand."

The drunken male squinted his eyes and swayed. He saw Ollie and company getting out of the water.

"Whaddaya think?" belched the seal, looking back at his female companions, wobbling. "He's got a raft of otters and a sea turtle with him."

Fandango saw the seals had piled kelp leaves within the small boat. One seal used an oar to stir the mess of whatever-it-was they were drinking. Seal after seal dipped their abalone shells into the dingy to gather more drink.

"There's plenty of kelp kooler for everyone," said a husky voiced female. "Besides, he looks like my type."

"Your type?" questioned the inebriated male. "This is my beach…"

And he collapsed, face first in the sand.

"That'll finish him for the night," said the female, as she turned an eye to Fandango. "Hey there, handsome stranger. Want some kelp kooler?"

The other seals hooted and hollered, hoisting up abalone shells and toasting, "May none of us get ring worm! Hip-hip, hooray!"

Fandango approached the party animals and saw their bubbling brew.

"Fermented kelp leaves, no?"

"Ripe from a day in the sun, you square shouldered sea biscuit," purred another female.

Several others sidled up to Fandango and one handed him a shell from which to drink. Fandango suddenly noticed that these were all female seals, except of course, for the lone male who had plowed face first into the sand.

"Beautiful ladies," wooed Fandango, "let us toast to the sunset in your sparkling eyes. Let us drink not only from cups, but also from love…"

"Think you're getting a little carried away there?" asked Ollie, having just hiked up the beach with the others.

"Ladies," yelled the proud Fandango. "Oh lovelies, meet my friends."

Fandango swilled his entire abalone shell of beach brew and bellow-burped after wiping his muzzle with a flipper.

"This is Ollie, Sadie, Browner, Fuzzy, and Ironhead. We have come and you are giving. Join in, my comrades. Drink up to our life worth living!"

"Uh, remember, we have to leave tomorrow," said Ollie.

"Ollie, Ollie, Ollie!" bellowed Fandango, after draining yet another abalone shell. "What is the rush, what is the hurry? Tomorrow will come and we shall have a choice, but tonight is ours, to have, to rejoice!"

"Oh, no," squawked Bingo. "He's gonna sing…"

Fandango began dancing with both female seals that hung onto his flippers.

FANDANGO: *"**A life worth livin'** the most important thing. To do it, to live it, ya gotta be, absolutely feeling free.*

The bold French seal swung a girl seal with each Flipper.

FANDANGO: *I'm just a party animal. Just a seal with zeal. There's nothing to feel bad about when it's love you feel!*

OLLIE: *You feel drunk.*

FANDANGO: *At least I'm not doing tricks for a meal. To do it, to live it, ya gotta be, absolutely feelin' free!*

The seals sang and danced wildly. Bingo squawked and flew out of harms way.

FANDANGO: *I'm just a party animal. Just a seal with zeal. There's nothing to feel bad about when it's love you feel!*

OLLIE: *Wine is fine, but you've had too much.*

FANDANGO: *I'm full of love and you know as such. To do it, to live it, ya gotta be, absolutely feelin' free! I'm just a party animal! Just a seal with zeal! There's nothing to be sorry about when it's love you feel!"*

Ollie, the other otters, Bingo, and Ironhead left the ongoing seal party and ventured down the beach. They settled at a cozy spot and pushed up a barricade of kelp and driftwood. The otters curled into balls, next to one another. Ironhead pulled his head and flippers into his shell, but he could still hear Fandango and the girl seals singing and dancing in the distance.

"Good night all," echoed Ironhead. "I sure had a good time

today."

Bingo waddled around within their kelp enclosure.

"Wouldn't ya know it. Everyone's cozy except for me."

"Shut your beak, please," said Ollie, wanting to sleep. "Just tuck your head into your chest feathers and call it a night."

"Just tuck my head into my chest feathers and call it a night?" grumbled Bingo. "What do ya think I am, a stinking sea bird?" Then he finally plopped his tail feathers down and made himself as cozy as he could.

Not far away the seals danced and drank kelp kooler long into the night until each one collapsed in the sand.

CHAPTER 15

Bombing Birds

Ollie woke up to the sound of rustling feathers. A gang of seagulls had invaded their camp in the middle of the night. Most of the gulls snored sporadic wheezes and their heads were tucked into their chest feathers. Bingo, the majestic blue macaw, nestled shoulder to shoulder with the flock of gray gulls.

"Great," complained Bingo, lifting up one of his talons and seeing seagull doo-doo on it. "Ya ask for something and ya get it."

Bingo threw open his wings, rudely waking up the seagulls.

"Ya dumb poop-dropping, sea-going birds! Don't you know where to do it and where not to do it!? Get outta here! Scram!"

The seagulls screeched and flew off.

"That's right, you heard me, buzz off!" commanded the proud macaw.

Bingo finally relaxed his tail feathers. But the flock of gulls banked in the air and turned back around.

"Uh-oh, they're circling back!" warned Bingo. "Duck!"

The otters hid under the kelp, just in time. Splat-splat-splat-splat, like machine gun fire came the seagull bombardment. Bingo became a wet, dirty mess, after being the bull's eye for the scorned squadron.

"You've got something in your eye!" screeched a fat gull.

"Yeah, now you're wearing yesterday's anchovy lunch!" chimed another seagull, and the entire flock cackled as they flew off.

"Smells like I better go for a swim and wash off," said Ironhead, not having fared much better than Bingo.

"I hate water!" crowed Bingo, furious. "That no good gang of gulls! I should've known better than to roost with the likes of them!"

Bingo trudged off to the surf. The otters came out from under their kelp protection, no worse for the wear.

"Let's round everybody up," said Ollie. "We better go before the Sea Park boat finds us."

CHAPTER 16

Fandango's Delusion

Ollie found Fandango asleep on the beach amidst the other hung-over seals.

"Fandango?"

"Mademoiselle?" groaned Fandango.

"It's me, Ollie. It's time to go."

Ollie thought the seals looked disgusting with their reddened eyes and kelp crusted muzzles.

"You all look like you washed up dead and smell just as bad. Pee-you."

"Ollie, this is my Otter Rock," said Fandango.

"No, it's not," challenged Ollie. "Otter Rock doesn't have a bunch of drunkards. It has seals with style."

"Ollie, your judgement hurts. These lovely ladies have befriended me. What can I do?"

"You can smell the sea breeze and wash your mouth out in a tide pool!" yelled Ollie. "How about that territorial male that passed out? Whaddaya think's gonna happen when he gets up? You've got a pot belly and flabby flippers. You're not ready for a fight!"

"Ollie, what can I say?"

"You're under their spell, Fandango. Listen to me. Otter Rock is a much better place. These seals probably beg tourists for French fries at the Crystal Cove pier. I can tell the kind of ladies they are."

"Tell him not to get his fur so bunched up," slurred a female seal that just woke up.

"Ollie, you are being disrespectful to my companions," said Fandango. "I must ask you to leave."

Ollie backed away, disappointed in his friend.

"Okay, Fandango. But I'm afraid your singing days are over."

CHAPTER 17

Bingo's Bad Day

Bingo preened his feathers meticulously clean in the ocean and chirped, "There, fresh as a baby macaw's bottom."

The local male seal woke up as Bingo passed by. The drunkard tried to shake his stupor off, flinging sand all over the poor bird.

"Ya big slobbering flea bag!" screeched Bingo. "I just took a bath! Seals, jaguars, and Watoobi warriors. Why'd God have to make them anyway?"

Once again, Bingo had to waddle to the water.

"Everybody ready?" asked Ollie, just arriving.

"Where's Fandango?" asked Sadie, as she played and wrestled with her two brothers in the surf.

"He's not coming."

"I ain't gonna cry about it, let me tell ya," squawked Bingo.

CHAPTER 18

The Only Way

Bingo flew high in the air keeping a bird's eye view of his friends below. The otters and Ironhead ate as they swam. Their method worked well. One of the otters swam ahead and by the time the others caught up, food was ready for them. A small flock of seagulls followed and squawked for food scraps. The Sea Park escapees swam in their leap frog fashion down the coast. Ollie kept looking for a landmark he might recognize to guide them to Otter Rock.

At one craggy section of shoreline they found an abundance of abalone. Fuzzy, Browner, and Sadie had learned how to successfully pry the abalone loose and eat the tasty mollusks.

Ollie and Sadie were snacking next to one another on the surface. Sadie dived down after one big red abalone she'd seen at the edge of a crevice. As she held her breath and banged a rock on the abalone, something suddenly grabbed her by the foreleg. It was a long, slithery creature and its jaws were like a vice grip. Sadie could not get away from it. The long creature wrapped around her and snarled from the cusp of its mouth.

"Errr, furrr food!"

Sadie fought to swim away from this thing but it had her tight and its teeth cut into her.

Meanwhile, Ollie leisurely picked another brown turban snail off his belly to eat as he coasted comfortably.

"You know Sadie, this is the life."

But there was no answer. Ollie looked to his right and noticed an abnormal flurry of bubbles. He knew that Sadie should have surfaced by now. Ollie rolled over and took a peek under the water.

Much to his horror he saw a large moray eel with its thick jaws attached to Sadie who was writhing and kicking to no avail. Ollie shot below the surface and dolphin-kicked down to the bottom.

"Let go of her!" demanded Ollie.

"Mind your own business or you'll be next!" retorted the eel.

"Ollie!" gasped Sadie, with a last breath.

The Only Way

Ollie knew there was only one thing he could do. He lunged at the base of the eel's head and bit into it. He chomped, gnashed and bit again until he felt only threads of sinew connecting the eel's head to its body. The long torso of the eel fell free, but decapitated jaws still gripped Sadie's foreleg. Sadie's body went limp. Ollie grabbed her and kicked to the surface with all of his might.

Sadie erupted at the top. Ironhead and Sadie's two brothers were right there to help. Ollie pushed Sadie on top of Ironhead where she expelled water from her lungs.

"What happened?" asked Fuzzy frantically.

"Is she okay?" yipped Browner.

Sadie couldn't talk and Ollie was too focused on her to respond. Finally, Sadie breathed as she coughed up one last trickle of sea water. Ollie managed to pry the moray eel's skull from her foreleg and heaved it to the seagulls that floated nearby. He watched as the seagulls attacked the dead head and fought one another for pecking rights.

"Yuck," said Ollie. "My dad taught me that's the only way to make a moray eel let go."

None of them said another word. But they all questioned themselves as to whether they should have remained in the safety of Sea Park.

CHAPTER 19

Party Animals

Back at the seal beach, Fandango and his new female friends got up and ventured into the surf for food. But no schools of herring or anchovies were close to the shore. The harem of seals didn't want to travel out far, to work hard for a meal. Instead, they settled for a snack of bulbous kelp floats close to the shore.

The decadent females convinced Fandango that they should finish off the kelp kooler or make more, before getting some food at the wharf.

"What do you mean, getting some food at the wharf?" asked Fandango.

"We're not talking about crabs and piling perch, that's for sure," answered the husky voiced female.

"French fries!" blurted a seal.

"And left over hamburgers!" shouted another female. "With sourdough bread. People even let us lick clam chowder out of a bowl."

"Ice cream, too!" yelped a third beauty.

The deep voiced female hung onto Fandango's flipper and sang in his ear.

"You're just a party animal..."

"Just a seal with zeal," bellowed another.

"Kelp kooler!" rallied a third seal. "C'mon!"

Several of the females grabbed hold of Fandango and sweet talked him into swimming. The seals rode a wave onto the beach, laughing and nipping at each other playfully.

"Last one to the dingy has to feed the kids!" barked the husky voiced female.

The seals raced up the beach to the dingy. Fandango was the first one there and collapsed in a heap, panting.

"Did you say kids?"

Suddenly, a horde of whelping sea lion pups scampered from out behind a fortress of rocks. There were dozens of them. They jumped on Fandango and licked him.

"But I'm a bachelor!"

"Go back to the den!" bellowed the territorial male, suddenly arising from the other side of the dingy.

The pups quickly scooted off.

"Well, what do we have here?" asked the jealous and now sober male. "A vagrant, that puts his flippers where they don't belong! Let's see how good you fling and sing after I get through with ya!"

The territorial male surprised Fandango by whacking him with an oar. The females cringed and turned their heads. They did nothing to help Fandango.

CHAPTER 20

Ollie's Little White Lie

Sadie was finally able to talk and said, "That thing, you bit its head off."

Ollie finished wrapping a kelp ribbon around her foreleg, as if it were a bandage.

"You saved my life, Ollie."

"There's so much that all of you have to learn," said Ollie. "It can be scary in the wild."

"It's a jungle out here, Kid," squawked Bingo.

"Maybe we should go back to Sea Park," said Fuzzy.

"Yeah," chimed Browner. "This living on the edge stuff is for the birds."

Bingo emitted a sharp squawk.

"You just have to pay attention," said Ollie. "You might not ever respect yourself back at Sea Park, as much as you would out here."

"What's respect?" asked Browner.

"The feeling you get when you're proud of yourself," answered Ollie. "Like when you get an abalone in deep water for the first time, on your own."

"Yeah, do ya wallow in a comfort zone or push the envelope?" asked Bingo, hovering nearby.

"What's an envelope?" asked Browner.

"Never mind," Bingo sighed.

Ollie looked up and saw something that captured his attention. The light house on the peninsula looked vaguely familiar. Then the marker buoy at the base of the light house clanged its bell loudly. Ollie recognized the distinct basso ring. He looked at the light house again and realized that the front of it faced Otter Rock.

"The light house! We're almost to Otter Rock!"

"Tonight?" asked Sadie, excited but exhausted.

Ollie gauged the distance as best he could.

"No. It's almost night time. We'll swim the channel to Otter Rock in the morning."

"Is the channel deep?" asked Browner.

"Yes."

"Great white sharks?" questioned Fuzzy.

"What's with you and sharks?" asked Ollie.

"They eat us!"

"Only if you think about them all the time," said Ollie impatiently.

Ollie considered what more he could say, or not say. He didn't want to make his friends scared before bed, but he also wanted to be honest.

"Don't worry about sharks," fibbed Ollie, biting his tongue. "They're mostly on the far side of Otter Rock."

CHAPTER 21

The Light House Tide Pools

The weary travelers were soon at the base of the light house. The surf pounded against the jagged shoreline. Ollie maneuvered his friends carefully and timed the crashing waves, so they wouldn't get bashed against the rocks.

"Now!" yelled Ollie, as a big swell crashed on the rocks violently, and they swam as fast as they could, parallel to the riptide, and into a protected tide pool.

From there it was easy to glide into shallower water. The tide pools would have some tasty tenders to eat before they went to bed. It was dark now.

"My flippers ache and I'm starved," complained Ironhead.

Ollie grabbed a sea star that was in easy reach.

"Here, Ironhead. Bite the tip off and suck out the stuff."

Ironhead nipped at the tip of the sea star and then drank up.

"Hmmm, not bad."

The otters found as many urchins as they wanted. There were even some shallow water black abalone to munch. Bingo landed on a large piece of driftwood and Ollie fetched him some sea grass to pick through.

"This greenery is super," whistled Bingo, as a strand of long sea weed dangled from his beak.

Ollie watched as each otter had their own way to eat an urchin. Sadie tapped hers lightly on a rock, many times, finally breaking off all the sharp spikes and fracturing the shell. Browner clobbered his against a rock, hard. The sharp spines flew and the shell cracked open, spilling out the roe. Sometimes he accidentally swallowed spine fragments as he ate the prized caviar.

Fuzzy hadn't quite developed his own urchin eating style and usually dropped his trying to bust it open. One time Fuzzy's urchin poked his paw and fell into the most interesting thing; an old tin can.

Fuzzy picked the can up from the bottom of the tide pool. The rusty container was almost as big as he was and there was something inside it.

"Put me down or I'll hex you and all your relatives," echoed the mysterious voice within the can. "And get this urchin off me."

The other otters also heard the strange voice and gathered around.

"Hex me and I'll put you down my throat!" replied Fuzzy.

"Go ahead and try, you half-baked otter," yelled the voice in the can.

"No problem!" responded Fuzzy, smacking his lips. "Come out, come out, whoever you are."

Suddenly, black ink squirted the furry otter's face.

"Ahhhh!" screamed Fuzzy. "I can't see!"

Fuzzy fell backwards and clutched his face with his rigid paws. Ollie doubled over laughing, because he knew what was in the can. Ollie simply washed sea water on Fuzzy's face and the little otter could again open his eyes.

"I told you not to mess with me," said the creature within the can. "And this is just the beginning!"

Ollie reached into the can and pulled out an ugly looking blob-creature, a rubbery invertebrate.

"You sure are feisty, for a sea slug."

"Put me down or else."

"Or else what?"

"Or else you'll all die!"

"Let's be real," reasoned Ollie. "How can you do that, to us?"

"Because I'm a gypsy sea slug, that's why!"

"A what?"

"That's right," said the slimy creature. "I'm a sea slug that interprets the tides, consults the depths – I can influence your mind!"

"What a bowl of bird guano!" squawked Bingo.

"I'd eat you, but you're no good anyway," said Ollie, tired of the slimy sea slug's talk.

The sea slug wouldn't stop his threats.

"Out there lays the deep channel. The Shark Channel. No marine mammal has crossed it alive. It is there that you will meet your doom!"

The eyes of all the animals lit up with fear, except for Ollie and Bingo.

"How'd the slug know we were going to swim the channel?" asked Browner, worried.

"Is it really called Shark Channel, Ollie?" asked Sadie.

"It is!" blurted the sea slug. "But he didn't tell you that for fear you wouldn't join him!"

"You talk too much!" yelled Ollie.

"Throw the slug over here, I'll peck its eyes out!" crowed Bingo.

"Wait!" shouted the Gypsy slug. "There's still time. Get me one shiny oyster pearl and I'll remove the death curse!"

"You don't scare me, even if you can read kelp leaves!" shot Ollie.

"You haven't answered my question, Ollie," demanded Sadie. "Is it called Shark Channel?"

Ollie stuffed the cosmic creature into the can.

"Yes, it's called Shark Channel. And the slug was right about me telling you that name. I thought you might get scared. But I never figured you wouldn't go with me."

"I don't want to swim where there's sharks," said Fuzzy.

"Neither do I," chimed Browner.

"We can get a pearl for the slug!" blurted Ironhead.

"Forget that," said Ollie. "I'm not letting a slimeball blackmail us."

"The slick slug just made a lucky guess. Don't worry about it," chirped Bingo.

"As you wish," slithered the slug. "A pearl you live. No pearl you die."

"C'mon everyone," said Ollie. "It's time to haul ashore and get some sleep. We've got a big day tomorrow."

Ollie took the can and placed it upside down at the bottom of the tide pool.

“That ought to shut that slug up.”

“Curse schmurse,” squawked Bingo.

The slug’s muffled threats and yelling were heard as they swam from the tide pool and into the big rocks on the shore.

“You’ll all die! The turtle will be soup! The rest of you will be eaten alive! Eaten alive I say! Unless of course, you let me out of this thing.”

CHAPTER 22

Fandango's Lesson

The local bull seal and his consorts had left Fandango to die. As they drank kelp kooler into the night, Fandango opened his swollen eyes. He tried to push himself onto his flippers, but fell. His shoulders were bloody from the oar beating and he couldn't support himself. Fandango knew he had to make it to the water. The salty sea would float his body and he could propel himself with his strong tail, that is, if he could make it. He tried to push himself up and again he fell, face first into the sand. He heaved and rolled. *Perhaps I can roll down the sandy incline,* he thought.

The drunken seals didn't notice Fandango's awkward escape as he somersaulted out of control into the surf.

Once in the water, Fandango felt some relief. The ocean water numbed his pain. Where would he go? He didn't have the strength to follow after his friends into unknown waters. He had to return to Sea Park; it might be his sole chance to survive. Kris could take care of him, nurture him, if only he could get that far.

Fandango felt good gliding in the water, hurting much less now that the cold night air wasn't stinging his open wounds.

Fandango realized Ollie was right. Those seals were no good. He spit into the ocean, trying to rid himself from the memory of that wretched bunch. He regretted trying to act like a young bull seal. He should have known better than to think that qualities of honor and true love could come from kelp kooler and a wild party. He berated himself for leaving Sea Park in the first place.

Fandango vowed to act his age; to learn his lesson. If only he would get another chance.

Sea Park was a long distance away and it was pitch black out. Fandango soon tired and realized he didn't have the strength to make it. He wasn't willing to pull up onto the shore to rest for fear that he would be taken advantage of by wild animals. *C'est la vie,* he thought. He would at least die in the ocean, trying. Having made that commitment, he felt his own self-respect again. He was thankful for having dared to live a free life.

Fandango lifted his head above the waterline and saw bright lights, not too far off. They nearly blinded him for a moment as the beams caught his face. Fandango realized the search lights were coming from a boat.

Fandango knew if the people on board were the bad kind of fishermen that he heard stories about, he might get killed. If the humans were the good kind, like Kris, they would save him, just as had happened when he was a pup and his fur was thick with spilt oil. Swimming to the boat was worth the risk for he would surely die in the water anyway.

Suddenly, Fandango heard the sweet sound of Kris' voice calling over the water, "Ollie? Fandango?"

The boat's spot light held on Fandango. Kris, Sasha and others were aboard.

"Fandango!" shouted Kris. She had tears in her eyes as she greeted the big seal. "Where have you been! Oh my God, what happened to you?"

Kris and Sasha lowered the dive ramp, helping Fandango onto it. "The others must be in the area," said Sasha.

Jim swiveled the antennae around trying to pick up Ollie's

radio signal. Fandango rested on the boat in a swath of towels and happily swallowed his hand fed fish while Kris tended his wounds.

"Fandango," said Kris. "You really did it this time."

The big seal put his head in her lap. *It was good to be alive,* he thought. *But I'll be smarter, next time.*

CHAPTER 23

Thinning of the Faithful

Two sea gulls squawked loudly, waking Ollie, as they fought over a small dead fish that had washed ashore. The little otter was the first to arise just as the sun dawned. Sadie, Fuzzy, Browner, Ironhead, and Bingo were still asleep.

Ollie quietly scampered into the tide pool and began looking for breakfast. He gathered an armful of sea urchins and brought them to his sleeping friends. Back in the tide pool he went for another load. He heard the sea slug mumbling inside the tin can. Ollie turned it over and quickly put his paw over the slug's mouth, stifling the doomsayer.

"Look, I'm going to let you go, because I'm a nice otter. I don't care about your darn curse. But if you get my friends scared again, I'll bite you in half and let the crabs pick you to pieces, got it?"

"Got it," mumbled the slug.

Ollie swam with the ugly invertebrate and tossed the slimy slug past the last tide pool into the ocean. The gypsy slug drifted away in the current.

"The curse will unfurl until I get the pearl!" shouted the slimy creature.

The slug's voice trailed off until it couldn't be heard as it drifted deeper into the sea. Ollie shook his head, thinking, *some animals just never learn.*

Ollie's friends were eating from their breakfast smorgasbord when he got back. Even Bingo was picking food from his sea salad.

"Thanks Ollie," said Sadie.

"Mmmm-hummm," sounded Fuzzy and Browner, nodding their heads, mouths full.

"I tossed and turned in my shell all night," said Ironhead. "I'm not going any further."

"Why?" asked Ollie, surprised. "Otter Rock's best for you, it really is."

"No, Ollie. Because of me, we haven't been able to swim fast.

I slow everybody down. Out there, in Shark Channel, I won't be any help. Maybe worse."

"That's not true, Ironhead," said Ollie.

"It is and you're kind to me, so you'll say anything to make me feel good. But I've made up my mind, Ollie."

"You're superstitious," squawked Bingo. "Ya let the gypsy slug get to ya."

"Please, Ironhead," begged Ollie.

"Sorry, Ollie."

"I'm going to miss you," said Ollie earnestly.

"Me too," chimed Sadie.

"Yeah," added Fuzzy.

"Maybe we should all stay with Ironhead!" shouted Browner.

"We can't settle for this place," said Ollie, taking in the scenery with a bland expression.

"We can go back to Sea Park," suggested Browner.

"I didn't learn one thing there," said Ollie.

"You could have learned a front-tuck flip, but you didn't practice!"

"I can do ten in my sleep," said Ollie, "if I wanted to. But why would you ever have to do a trick like that in the wild?"

No one answered him. Finally Browner piped up, "You just can't admit that you learned from us and someday it might come in handy."

"Well…" stammered Ollie.

"See, you can't admit you learned something from us."

"I can too. I learned that most humans are good. I wish Kris could be with us at Otter Rock."

"And Sasha," chimed Fuzzy.

"And Ironhead," added Sadie.

"Boo-hoo, boo-hoo," mocked Bingo. "All this baring of souls and good-bye stuff is killing me. Let's go before Lugnut changes his mind."

Ironhead submerged himself in the shallow tide pool feeling sad and worried for his friends.

CHAPTER 24

The Home Wrecker

Fuzzy and Browner swallowed nervously. One at a time the otters dived into the water. Bingo flapped his wings, catching a drift of air, and swooped over the waves.

There would be no casual back swimming. They were full and didn't want to dilly-dally in the channel. The otters swam on their bellies and bicycle-kicked for their one last marathon to Otter Rock.

Ironhead swam out of the last tide pool and watched his good friends leave. Normally sea turtles were steadfast once they made their minds up about something. But Ironhead clearly had second thoughts. It was sad for him to think he wouldn't see the little otters again, especially Ollie. Ironhead's stomach growled and he dived to the bottom, looking for something to eat. Wedged between two rocks, he saw the gypsy sea slug.

"Hey, a little help," said the stuck slug. "Wanna lend me a flipper?"

"As long as you don't put a curse on me."

"Deal. No curse."

The big turtle pushed on the sea slug, freeing the flexible invertebrate with a pop.

"Thanks a lot," said the slug. "But if it hadn't been for your pal, I wouldn't have got rock jammed in the first place."

"Say, I'd get you a pearl if I could," said Ironhead. "But I can't open oysters very well. Will you take your hex off my friends, since I helped you?"

"Hex schmex," laughed the sea slug. "I just made that up. I thought your otter pals might eat me. So, I used my gift of gab to get out of the situation."

Ironhead nudged the sea slug towards the two rocks where the ugly little creature was previously wedged.

"Hey, whaddaya think you're doing!" exclaimed the sea slug, as Ironhead jammed him between the rocks.

"Putting you in your place, you home wrecker!"

CHAPTER 25

Shark Channel

The otters noticed that the water had changed colors. Now it was dark blue with no apparent bottom.

"Why's the water so dark and spooky looking all of a sudden?" asked Fuzzy.

"The coastal shelf drop off," answered Ollie. "It's way deeper than an otter can swim."

It was eerie for Fuzzy, Browner, and Sadie to swim in water that seemed bottomless. Fuzzy's mind played tricks on him and he thought the slightest underwater shadow was a shark. The nervous otter bumped into Ollie repeatedly. Ollie grew irritated at Fuzzy's constant bumping and tried his best not to lash out in anger.

"Why are they called 'great whites', Ollie?" asked the nervous Fuzzy. "It'll make me less agitated if we talk about it."

"Because they have white on their stomachs," said Ollie.

"Oh."

"And they're kind of gray on top."

"If they come after you, do they circle around, like the sand sharks do with fish at the aquarium?" pestered Fuzzy, his paranoid eyes looking this way and that.

"You really want to know?" answered Ollie, as Fuzzy bumped him, for the fifty-fourth time.

"Yeah, yeah," blurted Fuzzy.

"They surprise you, when you're not paying attention and are bumping into everybody! That's when they swim up from underneath you and wham, you're dead tuna!"

Fuzzy nearly had a heart attack.

"Now get it out of your system!" commanded Ollie.

But that made the otters even more nervous and edgy. Their eyes scoured the depths below, hoping to see any sharks before the otter-eaters saw them.

"Shark!" screamed Browner suddenly.

The three domestics climbed all over Ollie.

"First of all," said Ollie calmly. "Panicking is not what you want to do. You have to stay strong and strategize. You have to separate and confuse the shark. Number two, that isn't a shark, it's a swordfish!"

The swordfish swam up to the raft of otters.

"What's a bunch of otters doing out here?" asked the swordfish.

"Just passing through," replied Ollie.

"Name's Nose," said the swordfish.

"Nice to meet you, Nose," responded Ollie.

But Ollie didn't want to stop and chat and kept his hindflippers kicking smoothly. Ollie saw the broadside of the swordfish. There was a huge half moon shaped scar on its side. Ollie knew it was from the bite of a great white. Ollie wondered how the swordfish had gotten away, with a bite mark so big.

"I've got some flotsam up ahead that attracts squid and fish," said Nose. "Want me to spear you some?"

"No thanks," replied Ollie, not feeling good about this swordfish for some reason.

"It's no problem, really," persisted Nose.

"I am kind of hungry, Ollie," said Browner.

"Yeah, me too," added Fuzzy.

"Sure, take a break," said Nose. "It's a crab crate, floating just up ahead. You can have a quick rest and I'll have your food on my spear by the time you get there."

"Gee, thanks," said Fuzzy.

"Yeah," added Browner.

"Don't mention it," said the swordfish. "I'm glad to help fellow travelers making their way." Nose darted off into the depths with a whoosh of his tail.

"He seemed awfully nice," said Sadie.

"I don't know," cautioned Ollie.

"There's the crate!" yelled Browner.

They watched as Nose shot under the floating crate, scattering a school of squid. The swordfish impaled a dozen of the tentacle-creatures on his spear and swam over to the otters, offering them lunch.

"Here ya go, help yourselves."

Browner and Fuzzy greedily pulled off a few squid and ate them up. Sadie took a couple as well and handed one to Ollie. Ollie still didn't feel comfortable with this swordfish named Nose, but gobbled down the tasty squid, anyway.

"There's some crabs in the crate that you can have as well," said Nose.

"All right," said Fuzzy.

"Yeah," said Browner.

"Gee thanks," said Sadie, thinking Ollie was being unfair to this generous swordfish.

"C'mon," offered Nose. "Hang out at the crate for a minute and we'll get you one last delicious snack before you're on your way."

The otters swam to the floating-crate full of crabs. It was a large wooden crate with at least a dozen king crabs inside it. A rope trailed the crate, having been severed from a marker buoy.

Ollie brought up the rear. He worried that his otter friends had gotten too excited and weren't paying attention, a setup for trouble.

Nose introduced Sadie, Fuzzy, and Browner to his two jellyfish pals that kept an eye on his crate.

"This is Kilo and that's Watt. They watch my crate and I pay 'em in bottom fish."

The otters were mesmerized by the translucent beauty of the two Man-o-Wars. The strange looking creatures had long string-like legs dangling far underneath them. Even Ollie had never seen jellyfish like this before. Ollie paid them no mind, because he was more concerned about a surprise shark attack.

"Reach into the crate and help yourself to those crabs," suggested Nose.

"Yeah," encouraged Kilo.

"They've been bugging us anyway with their dumb escape

plans," added Watt.

"Gee thanks," said Fuzzy.

"Love to," said Browner.

"I'm starved," said Sadie.

The three otters reached their paws into the crate. Kilo and Watt winked at each other.

"Now!" cackled Nose.

The two jellyfish dropped their stinging tendrils on the otters. Sadie, Browner, and Fuzzy screamed out in pain from the electrical shocks. The more the otters fought, the more they got tangled in the stingers. The chemical voltage paralyzed the otters; they could not move or talk.

Ollie swam around, his adrenaline pumping.

"Hey? What's going on?!"

Nose spoke from the side of his mouth, "These little otters are live bait for Tooth! Kilo and Watt, float them to the top before the furry things drown! I'll tell the boss lunch is served!"

"You slimy swordfish!" shouted Ollie, as Nose disappeared into the depths.

Kilo and Watt floated their stinging tentacles to the surface. The otters popped to the waterline like corks, dazed and unable to move, but at least breathing.

"Let go of my friends," shouted Ollie.

"Why don't you come closer, little otter," said Kilo, laughing a wicked cackle.

"When Tooth comes, we'll let your friends go," sneered Watt. "They'll twitch around on the surface and old Fang Face will eat them whole!"

"Or bite them in half!" exclaimed Kilo.

"It's kind of gross to watch," commented Watt. "Old Tooth getting blood in the water and all. But it beats floating around doing nothing."

"So, it's Tooth!" exclaimed Ollie, with a measure of fear and loathing.

"Who did you expect, the Little Mermaid?" laughed Watt wickedly.

"What's he paying you to be his stooges?" asked Ollie. "I'll double it if you let them go, now!"

"It's an interesting proposition," said Kilo. "Except, we've got a contract with the big guy, already."

"I'll push an entire school of herring your way," begged Ollie.

"Hmmm," sighed Watt. "That's enticing. But our arrangement is such that if we don't snooker mammals into our grasp, then Tooth eats us. In fact, had you not come along, we would have been lunch!"

So, that was why Nose had a huge shark bite-scar on his side, thought Ollie. *Tooth probably let the swordfish go in exchange for becoming a stooge for him.*

Ollie swam to the surface and breathed deep the air. Bingo was sitting on top of the crate, preening himself.

"What's with our buddies, they look a little zapped."

"They are zapped!" shouted Ollie. "The jellyfish stung them and they can't move! Tooth the great white shark is coming to eat them!"

"Yikes!" shouted Bingo. "Why didn't ya tell 'em to stay away from the jellyfish in the first place?!"

"I was keeping lookout and I didn't grow up in the deep water, you know!"

"What can we do?" asked Bingo.

"I don't know!"

Ollie swam around the crate, looking for an angle, an idea, some sort of way out.

"Then they're doomed," crowed Bingo.

CHAPTER 26

Tooth

Tooth was so named because of a deformity on his lower jaw which caused a row of his serrated teeth, and particularly one big one, to jut from his mouth like a gargantuan, jagged saber.

Tooth was leisurely picking his teeth with some driftwood down in the depths when Nose arrived with the good news.

"Boss!" exclaimed Nose. "Have I ever got a surprise for you!"

"It better be good, pencil nose," said the monster shark impatiently. "I was just thinking that swordfish was on the menu today."

"You're gonna do a lot better than that boss!" gulped Nose nervously. "Oh yeah! How does three warm blooded otters sound?"

"Otters," blasted Tooth, bringing his mighty jaws just inches from Nose's face. "Don't kid me. They're my favorite and I haven't clipped an otter spine in quite awhile!"

"Really, Boss," whined Nose. "There are three of 'em, just waiting for you!"

Nose heard a loud rumbling noise from Tooth's big belly.

"What's that sound, boss?"

"My tapeworm just woke up," said Tooth casually. "Let's go! Show me the sweet meat!"

And the big shark laughed a hideous laugh that sent shock waves through the ocean.

"Ha, ha-ha-ha, haaa!"

CHAPTER 27

No Way Out

Ollie and Bingo had examined every part of the crate. The situation looked hopeless.

"Uh-oh," said Ollie to Bingo. "Hear that?"

"Hear what?"

"Tooth's on his way. I've heard that laugh before."

"Then I gotta let my feathers down and tell ya what you're not gonna want to hear," squawked Bingo.

"What?" asked Ollie.

"Ya gotta scram, Ollie. If the big shark comes, you'll be the first one he goes after. He'll know he has the others when he wants them."

"No!" blurted Ollie. "I'm not leaving Sadie! I'm not leaving Fuzzy and Browner!"

"Let me talk some sense into you, please," crowed Bingo. "There's nothing we can do! Even I know an otter can't just bite through a jellyfish's stinging tentacles!"

"Jellyfish?" asked a familiar voice. "Did someone say jellyfish?"

Ironhead appeared from behind them and patted Ollie's back with a flipper.

"Ironhead!" shouted Ollie. "Can you eat jellyfish?"

"Ollie, they're my favorite. Only us sea turtles can eat jellyfish."

"Then bite the scummy legs off these two criminals!" shouted Ollie. "They've zapped our friends!"

Kilo and Watt looked at each other at the same time and said, "Uh-oh."

Ironhead swam into the jellyfish tendrils and bit into the long stringy legs, slurping them down like they were strands of licorice. The bodies of the Men-o-Wars no longer had tentacles attached.

"Ahhh!" groaned Kilo and Watt. "We're nothing now! Just a couple of floating blobs!"

Ironhead made further passes and gobbled up all of the jellyfish tendrils. The captured otters were suddenly able to open their eyes and feel their limbs again, but were still in shock. Ollie swam Sadie to the crate.

With Bingo's help, they got her safely on top, out of the water. One by one, Ollie rescued Fuzzy and Brown Nose. But the paralyzed otters still couldn't respond.

Ollie knew Tooth would arrive in thundering fashion, any second. The mighty shark could easily knock his helpless friends off the crate and into his jaws.

"Ironhead!" shouted Ollie, "You've got to tow this thing! Here, let me put the rope over your head!"

Ironhead maneuvered to the front of the crate and Ollie swam the rope over to him. Ollie quickly tied it around Ironhead's upper shell.

"Just like at Sea Park," said Ollie. "Only go faster!"

"I'll try!" exclaimed Ironhead, feeling more important now than he ever had in his life.

Bingo flew into the air, keeping lookout for Tooth.

"Ya saved their lives, ya big Leather Neck. I'll never say anything bad about ya again!"

Ironhead smiled, knowing it was hard for Bingo to say anything nice to anybody. The Turtle pulled with his flippers as hard as he could. The entire flotilla began moving.

"One, two, stroke," said Bingo, keeping cadence. "One, two,

stroke. One, two, stroke."

Underwater, Ollie's eyes searched the dark depths for Tooth.

Never had an otter survived an encounter with Tooth. In fact, they were usually swallowed whole on the first bite. The thought of which made Ollie cringe.

The little otter mustered up his courage and told himself he could elude Tooth. He would be the first otter to survive, and so would his dear friends. Ollie felt strong again, his eyes ever watchful. He thanked the Deep Blue Sea that he'd made it this far and for his feeling of confidence.

It's now a matter of destiny, Ollie said to himself. *An otter's gotta do what an otter's gotta do*.

CHAPTER 28

Show Down at High Noon

"One, two, stroke," squawked Bingo. "One, two, oh-no!"

Bingo saw a huge dorsal fin cutting the surface of the water. It was Tooth, and the mighty shark was bigger than even Bingo imagined.

Tooth, with his factory of teeth, was narrowing the distance to the crate. Bingo had to tell Ollie, but how? The little otter was under the water. Bingo realized what he had to do. He had to power dive into the sea like a pelican and get Ollie's attention. Bingo *hated* getting wet.

"The things I gotta do," mumbled the mad macaw. "Bravo

Louie-Code Red, *extreme macho!*"

The indigo-blue macaw swooped into a power dive, wings tucked. He felt his tiny facial feathers buffet from the G-force stress and hit the water like a real sea bird. A plumb of water burst up into the air. Bingo shot beneath the surface as if he were an Amazon torpedo.

Startled from Bingo's splash, Ollie's heart nearly jumped out of his furry chest. He saw Bingo's puffy cheeks as the bird pointed frantically at something behind Ollie.

Ollie snapped his head quickly and saw the fierce and pointed shape of the giant Tooth bearing down on them. For an instant Ollie froze. He felt a fire of fear within himself which locked his muscles rigid. Bingo squawked under the water and brought Ollie to full attention. Ollie squeezed his forepaws into firm otter fists, wakened to action. He shot to the surface and filled his lungs with as much as air as they would hold.

Bingo floundered to the top and gasped. With the little strength he had left, the exotic bird dragged his wet feathers aboard the crate.

Ollie slapped his hindflippers on the water's surface several times, knowing that Tooth would hear the sound. The desperate otter dived and darted away from the crate.

"Hey Tooth! Your breath smells like whale poop!"

Tooth veered towards Ollie. Nose flanked the mighty Shark.

"That's the one that didn't get zapped," said the stooge swordfish. "The others are ready for you now."

Tooth had Ollie in his sights and his mighty jaw etched a sinister smile.

"I can have the others for dessert. The smart aleck is my appetizer!"

"Gotta bring help, huh Tooth?" asked Ollie. "Getting old or something?"

And the little otter swam further away from the crate.

"Old and hungry!" bellowed Tooth with his wicked laugh. "Ha, ha-ha-ha, haaaa!"

Up on the crate, Bingo splashed water on the faces of the dazed otters.

"C'mon ya little space cadets. Wake up!"

The otters could hear Bingo and see him, but they didn't have control of their muscles yet, try as they might.

Bingo yelled to Ironhead, "Stroke-stroke-stroke-stroke-stroke-stroke!"

Ollie swam as fast as he could but looked behind and saw Tooth clearly gaining on him. Ollie knew that he wasn't as fast a swimmer as a streamlined great white. Ollie had the stamina, but not the speed or strength. He had to make the mighty shark miss him; that would be his only chance.

Tooth thrust powerfully, building up to full velocity attack mode.

Suddenly, Ollie stopped swimming. He turned and faced Tooth squarely.

"Okay you win," said Ollie. "But man, you are ugly."

"Swim you little table scrap!" demanded Tooth.

"What for?"

"I see your point," said Tooth. "Very well, down the hatch."

The mighty great white opened his jaws showing row upon row of serrated teeth and red gristle. One huge fang protruded from his mouth like a death spike.

Ollie hovered in the water with his tail up flat against his belly and his eyes were closed. Ollie looked resigned to his fate. Then he risked a quick peek…

Ollie saw Tooth open his big mouth all the way, unhinging the cartilage jaw for a massive chomp. Tooth's eyes rolled and turned a deathly black. Ollie suddenly flipped his tail downward as hard as he could. The front-tuck flip carried the little otter upwards in a somersault, just over Tooth's upper jaw. Tooth bit down with a clash of knives so hard that he lost a few teeth.

Nose swam at Tooth's side and said, "I've never seen an otter do that, boss."

"Neither have I or he'd be sweet meat between my teeth, you fool!"

"Nothing but a front-tuck flip, fellas," said Ollie. "Sea Park tricks of the trade."

Tooth had to make a wide turn to get his large frame moving in the other direction. Ollie popped up to the surface. He saw Bingo trying to revive the otters. He could also see Otter Rock in the distance. Ollie took a few deep inhalations and gently slipped below the surface.

"Sorry, Tooth," said Ollie. "I hope you hadn't worked up an appetite."

"See funny otter die!" snarled Tooth, as the behemoth powered towards Ollie.

Ollie suddenly bolted, narrowing the angle between himself and Tooth.

"Pull up, Boss!" directed Nose.

"Aaarrrggghhh!" thundered Tooth loudly, trying to shorten his attack angle on Ollie.

Ollie passed over Tooth's top jaw and the humungous shark

broke through the surface like a breaching humpback whale. Tooth's powerful tail thrashed at the water as he tried to propel downwards towards the escaping otter. Ollie was surprised at how fast Tooth recovered. The huge great white came at him again.

"I lost my sense of fairness when I missed you the first time!" railed Tooth, more angry than ever. "Nose, corral him for me!"

The swordfish was one of the fastest fish in the ocean, much faster than an otter. A paralyzing fear enslaved Ollie, but the little otter forcefully shook his head, thinking forcefully, *I'm brave right now!*

Once again, Ollie experienced his otter courage. He swam with all his might, refusing to think of a ghastly finale. He shot downwards into the depths.

Nose caught up and swam ahead of Ollie.

"Going someplace, otter chow?"

"To your funeral!" shouted Ollie, bubbles trailing from his mouth.

Tooth bore down on Ollie and the otter saw the mighty jaws open, the eyes already rolling back. *Uh-oh*, Ollie thought, *he's in his final lunge!*

Tooth was too close for Ollie to flip away. Ollie tried to push ahead to get more distance between them, but Nose hovered directly in front of Ollie and held the otter in check with his sharp spear. Ollie was trapped.

On one side he could see the ugly-red innards of Tooth's mouth and on the other, the razor sharp spear of Nose. There was no room to go up, down or to the side, without getting bitten in half or harpooned.

Ollie suddenly spun himself towards Nose with a thrust from his forepaws. Ollie timed his move perfectly as he twisted his skinny body to the side of the swordfish's spear. The long and sharp staff grazed Ollie's thick fur as he slid to the side. Tooth chomped down and Nose's saber penetrated the back of Tooth's mouth, stabbing deep into the monster shark's brain.

Tooth's jaws collapsed on the spear. Ollie was so close, he could have touched the large fang on Tooth's deformed jaw if he wanted. One of Tooth's eyes stared at Ollie, black and lifeless. All forward motion stopped. Tooth and Nose sank as the mighty great white's body spasmodically quivered.

Tooth was dead.

Nose's spear had impaled itself deeply within the dead great white shark. The sinister swordfish was stuck. Nose tried to pull away but couldn't.

"Little otter. Have mercy. Help me!"

"There's nothing I can do. You're too big and heavy for me to pull you out. Plus you were bad."

"Please, I'm begging you…"

Ollie watched as the evil duo sank into the blackness that appeared to have no end. Finally it was silent in the cold, dark Pacific.

Ollie swam to the surface that sparkled like diamonds. He now felt as if he were floating in a warm current, protected by the Deep Blue Sea. He wondered for a moment why it was he that got to live. When would his destiny become less fortunate?

Gotta stay positive, said Ollie to himself, not wanting to dilute his marvelous feeling of the moment. *And thanks to the Deep Blue Sea.*

CHAPTER 29

Return to Otter Rock

Ironhead towed the crate into a cove at Otter Rock. Sadie, Fuzzy and Browner were finally moving about. Bingo flew in the air and Ollie swam, floating on his back, leisurely kicking his flippers.

"When Tooth came flying out of the water, and I mean flying, I thought for sure you were a goner!" exclaimed Bingo. "Whew! This ain't no Disney movie!"

"Wait until all the otters at Otter Rock hear that you killed Tooth, Ollie," barked Sadie. "You'll be famous."

"Famous, schmamous," squawked Bingo. "He'll be a legend. They'll make sand statues of him. They'll sing songs about him.

"Okay, okay," said Ollie. "But, they won't believe it. A rumor once went around that Tooth was dead. And it wasn't true. They won't believe it this time. Anybody hungry?"

"I am!" exclaimed Browner.

"Me too!" shouted Fuzzy.

"All this towing has got me hungry," said Ironhead.

"How 'bout a little sea grass salad, Ollie?" chirped Bingo, flying low.

"Coming right up," said Ollie.

Ollie rolled over onto his belly and dived below the water's surface, leaving a trail of white bubbles behind him. Strangely, there were no ribbons of kelp. There was no sea grass or urchins, just a few scattered starfish that clung to rocks. The bottom looked naked, ghostlike. Some small bottom fish darted in the rocks, in and out of the streaks of sunshine, but there were no large fish.

Ollie surfaced and looked to the shore. Where were the sea lions? Where were the otters and the sea birds that roosted on the cliffs? The Sea Park escapees were close to the shore now and should have seen creatures teaming the tiny beach.

"What's the matter?" asked Sadie, knowing that something was wrong.

"Where is everyone?" answered Ollie with a question of his

own. "That's what's wrong. There should be hundreds of seals and otters. Birds used to be everywhere. The kelp's gone. There's no urchins or anything!"

Ollie was becoming frantic.

"Bingo! Fly up high and tell me if you see otters on the other side!"

Bingo flew quickly, catching a leeward draft, and glided up and over the low cliffs of Otter Rock. He could see down below to the crashing surf on the shore, unprotected against the harsh Pacific. There were no animals. There was no kelp.

Bingo flitted back down to the raft as Ironhead's flippers touched the sand bottom. Sadie, Browner, and Fuzzy jumped off. Ollie was already ashore, staring out over the water, defeated.

"Nothing, zip, finito," said Bingo.

"I know," replied Ollie, depressed. "They'd never live over there. Too much wind. No caves. Sorry I made you look."

"Anytime, Kid," said Bingo, draping a wing over Ollie's shoulder.

Bingo felt the little otter's body tremble. Ollie collapsed in the sand.

"They're gone!" wept Ollie. "It's all gone. That giant eel and the red faced man took everything!"

"What's he crying about?" asked Browner.

"Will ya let him have his moment for Pete's sake?" answered Bingo.

"Bingo, who's Pete?" asked Ironhead.

"Sheesh," sighed Bingo, wondering how Ironhead ever got this far in life.

Bingo patted Ollie on the back.

"The Kid's still the champ of the world, ain't he?" said Bingo, looking at all the animals.

"Of course he is," said Sadie proudly. "He saved our lives."

"But now we'll starve to death on this dead world," blurted Ollie. "And it's all my fault!"

CHAPTER 30

The Dark Night at Otter Rock

Night fell and the animals curled up together. The wind howled and blew bone cold. The sound of the ocean waves echoed against the palisades behind them. They were tired and hungry, and for all they knew, tonight would be their last.

"We wouldn't be in this position had we stayed in the safety and comfort of Sea Park," said Fuzzy.

"Yeah," chimed Browner. "Learning self-respect is one thing, dying is another."

Ollie's head hung low and he didn't refute their comments.

"Then you should never have came," said Bingo. "I've watched you little fur balls grow up more in the past week than your entire lives. Better to live a life worth living and die with dignity than to be dumb and happy."

"I'd take dumb and happy right now," croaked Browner.

"Respect yourself and you won't die, on the inside at least," said Bingo.

"Oh that's a good one," said Browner.

"Bingo's right," said Sadie.

"How's respecting yourself going to help us, now?" asked Fuzzy.

"I don't know, exactly," said Sadie. "But Ollie's taught us that confidence and commitment creates good luck. And we can at least thank the Deep Blue Sea for what we've got."

"That isn't much," groaned Browner.

"We've got each other," said Ironhead. "Isn't that why we left Sea Park?"

"I feel more confidence than I ever have before," said Sadie. "Even though it's been scary."

The wind howled and kicked up a flurry of sand. The animals huddled together tightly. Before long, they had all fallen asleep. Ollie's last thoughts were of the sparkling plankton in the Deep Blue Sea.

CHAPTER 31

Surprise Visit

The animals woke up to the sound of an airplane flying overhead. Little did they realize that it was a search plane that had picked up Ollie's transmitter signal. The plane called in a finding report to the search boat below, which had been canvassing the channel.

Not long after the circling plane left, the Sea Park expedition boat slid into the cove, very close to the shore. A seal barked loudly, and people shouted:

"OLLIE? SADIE?"

"Hey!" squawked Bingo. "It's the King of kelp kooler himself."

The other sleepy-eyed and hungry animals startled. The sight of Kris, Sasha, Fandango, and other Sea Park people relaxed their worried hearts; Kris would take care of them, even if it did mean going back to Sea Park.

All of them, except for Ollie, dashed as quickly as they could to the boat. Kris called out each of their names, greeting them one by one, and giving each animal food.

Fandango wore bandages all over himself. When the otters asked him what happened, he said he didn't want to talk about it, but that he was better off, in the long run, than the other seal.

Kris walked up the beach and found Ollie by himself.

"Hey Ollie, what's the matter?"

Ollie placed his sad face into her lap.

"A lot of otters used to live out here," said Kris. "But an illegal harvester came in and took away all the food. Maybe this was your home, Ollie. Is that why you came here?"

Ollie nodded his head.

"You always seem to know what I'm saying," added Kris. "But you don't look too happy. Let me take you back to Sea Park, Ollie."

Ollie stared back at Kris with sad eyes that penetrated to her heart.

"Don't give me such a look, Ollie. But at least you're okay."

But Ollie held his solemn gaze, still and focused. Kris looked deeply into Ollie's eyes and her thoughts went into slow motion. She remembered, strangely enough, her father. Then another memory conjured up from her past. It was a vision of the group of otters that she trained and released in the wild, that died.

"Ollie," said Kris. "Maybe you're not ready to be released. I can't let anything bad happen to you."

Ollie pawed at her, his eyes pleading.

"I can't let you go, Ollie, until I'm sure you can handle it."

Ollie muzzled his nose against her throat. Kris felt for the pearl necklace that she once wore as Ollie squirmed and looked up at her.

"Okay," said Kris. "Maybe you know better than I do what's best for you. It's not like there's a formula for releasing otters back to the wild."

CHAPTER 32

Home in a Strange Place

The Sea Park boat bounced over the ocean swells. Ollie couldn't believe how fast it traveled. It was one thing to see boats zip over the water, it was another to be aboard one and feel the sensation of speed. The boat headed south, away from Sea Park and Otter Rock.

Ollie felt better, because he knew his friends were safe, yet he remained unsettled. It was a relief that Kris arrived, saving them from starvation on the now desolate Otter Rock. Yet, despite his gratitude for their rescue, Ollie knew his hankering for a free life would not end. He could never be happy at Sea Park.

The boat skipped along a large patch of kelp. Ollie saw how

beautiful it looked, how lush. He hadn't seen kelp like this since his old days at Otter Rock. He saw a seal in the water, then more seals. A flock of pelicans skimmed over the water. Ollie's little ears pricked up as he took it all in carefully. Kris noticed. She smiled, knowing she made the right decision.

Ollie saw otters frolicking in the kelp. He got so excited that Kris had to contain him until the boat slowed down. The boat hadn't even come to a complete stop when Kris finally said, "Okay, okay!"

Kris let go of Ollie. The otter jumped from the boat and into the water. Kris and the others watched eagerly as Ollie swam up to a raft of otters and mingled with them immediately.

"I wonder what they're saying to each other?" asked Kris of no one in particular.

CHAPTER 33

Ollie's Gift to Kris

Ollie playfully hit a young male otter with his paw.

"The day you dodge a great white and live to talk about it, is the day you'll be able to dive deeper than me!"

"Get out of here," said Ollie's friend. "You did not."

"Did too. Want me to give you an otter noogie?"

"You can't spell noogie."

Ollie wrestled with his friend as an adult male and female raced through the kelp canopy towards them. Kris watched from the boat, concerned.

"Uh-oh. Older male moving in. Could be a territorial dispute about to happen."

The older male and female tackled Ollie and all three rolled over and over in the kelp canopy, hugging and nipping at each other.

"Mom! Dad!" shouted Ollie excitedly.

"Ollie!" yipped Ollie's mom with joy. "Ollie came back to us! Oh, thank the Deep Blue Sea!"

Kris relaxed. At first she thought they were fighting. But it was quickly obvious that the two adults liked this special little otter.

"Okay," said Kris. "Who else wants to go?"

Bingo flew from his perch on the boat and landed on a rock near some pelicans.

"Hey guys. Ya think a macaw like me can fit in out here?"

"Get real," said one of the pelicans, as if Bingo was a disease.

The pelican whacked Bingo with the back side of a big, brown wing, sending Bingo end over end into the water. Bingo looked up, spitting a kelp float from his beak. Seaweed draped his head.

"Hey pelican pea-brain! Didn't your parents teach ya any manners?"

The pelicans pointed their wing tips at Bingo and laughed.

"This oceanic wild life is for the birds," grumbled Bingo.

Bingo flapped away the kelp and flew back to the boat.

"Don't worry, Bingo," said Kris. "I still love you."

"I still love you," repeated Bingo. "I still love you."

The three domestic otters lined up on the bow of the boat. Ollie swam over with a raft of his friends.

"C'mon in Sadie," said Ollie. "I want you to meet my mom and dad and some buddies of mine!"

"I don't know…" said Sadie, feeling nervous.

Ollie whispered to a couple of his pals and the friends dived under the water.

"Why not?" asked Ollie. "This is our paradise."

"But Kris had to save us!"

"Sadie, you're going to love it here!" exclaimed Ollie.

Sadie looked at her two brothers, who inched backwards, towards the safety of Kris.

"Guys?" asked Sadie.

"It looks fun but I'm scared," said Fuzzy.

"Me too," chimed Browner.

Ollie's wild otter friends surfaced and handed him something. Ollie swam closer to the boat.

"The jellyfish nearly killed us, Ollie," said Sadie. "I can't begin to say what that felt like, not being able to move or talk."

Ollie lifted up both of his forepaws. He cradled a white pearl that shined pink in spots as the sunlight kissed it.

"For me?" asked Sadie.

Ollie nodded his head.

"You are my pearl, Ollie," said Sadie.

Sadie looked at Kris, barked sweetly, and gestured at Ollie's offering. Kris took the pearl from Ollie.

"One last trick, huh Ollie? We'll never have another otter like you at Sea Park."

Sadie dived into the water. As did Fuzzy and Brown Nose. Ironhead beat his flippers on the deck of the boat, so Kris and Sasha shoved the heavy turtle over board. Kris, Sasha, their trainer friends, Bingo, and Fandango, watched them go.

At one point, Kris swore to Sasha that Ollie actually said goodbye to her from the kelp. Sasha laughed, saying Kris had identified with the animals a bit too much.

"I swear he's half human," said Kris.

Ollie rafted with his clan of otters that included his family, old friends, and the newcomers.

"I swear she's half otter," Ollie said, regarding Kris.

The otters laughed at Ollie, telling him it was because he liked the human so much.

"So, what do you think?" asked Sasha.

"This time it's going to work," said Kris, clutching the pearl tightly in her hand. "They're going to adapt and thrive."

Bingo cocked his head. The yellow-ringed eyes of the proud hyacinth macaw reflected dual images of one very special friend.

"Ollie the otter," squawked Bingo, as loudly and majestic as he could muster. "Ollie the otter. Ollie the otter."

THE END

Talking Critters™ series

www.cherubsplay.com

or

www.ollietheotter.com

Where kids and critters talk from the heart

To order more copies of

Ollie the Otter:

Go to our Web site and order away! We link you directly to the best on-line bookseller to give you great service and secure transactions.

IT'S AS EASY AS RAFTING IN KELP!

BUT THEY DON'T ACCEPT ANCHOVIES OR INNKEEPER WORMS!

Visa
MasterCard
Discover
American Express

I THINK THESE PEOPLE DESERVE EXTRA POOL TIME AND FRESH SQUID!
JUST SWIM TO THE NEXT PAGE TO SEE THEIR NAMES...

Credits

Author: **Kelly Alan Williamson**

Publisher: **Cherubs Play**

Otter photographer, front cover, front & back flaps: **Richard Bucich**

Great white shark and otter photographer, back cover: **Alan Studley**

Typesetting & layout : **Peri Poloni**

Cover design: **Peri Poloni**

Editors: **Bobi Martin, Zoe Elton, and Christina Williamson**

Shark photo graphics work: **Bob Centilli**

Digital photo processing: **A1 Photography**

Logo work: **Steve Rottblat**

Book Printer: **United Graphics' Jill Lansdale,**
Bridget Pierce, and Brenda Neff

Ollie song hip-hop beat: **David Freiberg**

The Sea Park Band Singers:
Jessie Williamson, Katie Schmidt, Megan McNay, and Emily Hunt

Pre-press manuscript copies: **The Copy Corner's**
Randy Guerrieri and Team

HEY,
YOU WANT TO ROCK IN THE WAVES WITH THE SEA PARK BAND? GO TO MY WEB SITE. LISTEN TO US CROONING IN THE KELP!
www.ollietheotter.com
OR FLAP YOUR FLIPPERS TO THE NEXT PAGE AND START SINGING NOW!

The Ollie Song

Ollie the otter,
'most wonderful little guy.
He frolics in the ocean waves,
'might spit you in the eye!

Ollie the otter,
'rough and tumble lad.
He swims and dives for turban snails,
'latest teenage fad!

Ollie the otter,
'loves to dance in kelp.
He laughs and plays with otter friends,
'always there to help!

Refrain: OLLIE-OLLIE, OLLIE THE OTTER!
OLLIE-OLLIE, OLLIE THE OTTER!

Ollie the otter,
'had to be set free.
He loves his spunky trainer Kris,
'first love is the sea!

Ollie the otter,
'not scared of any shark.
He knows the ocean can be rough,
But he's 'full of otter spark!

Ollie the otter,
'loves his Sea Park friends.
Fandango, Bingo and Sadie,
'their fun never ends!

Refrain: OLLIE-OLLIE, OLLIE THE OTTER!
OLLIE-OLLIE, OLLIE THE OTTER!

SEE YA LATER
BUT DON'T SAY GATOR!
REPTILES GIVE ME
THE CREEPS!